THE HUNTER

THE ARACHNOID CHRONICLES: BOOK TWO

D.C. BROCKWELL

any resemblance to actual persons, living or dead, business establishments, events, or locales is purely coincidental unless used to add historical perspective.

ISBN: 9798837843709

❀ Created with Vellum

1

Jenna Martin had never felt pain like it before. Her belly was on fire. Lying on a hospital gurney in the accident and emergency department at Queen Mary Hospital, Roehampton Lane, Jenna prayed the doctor would present himself, and soon. Trying her hardest not to squirm on the crinkly sheets beneath her, she closed her eyes, trying to think what might be troubling her enough to give her stomach cramps.

Being of a nervous disposition never helped matters of the stomach, Jenna had been brought up by two perfect parents. Or at least they thought they were perfect anyway. Her dad was a leading psychiatrist in his field, a true academic, the smartest man Jenna knew. While her mum was a leading physician, but luckily not at Queen Mary's. Or was that unlucky for Jenna? She might have been seen sooner. Having two such intelligent and overpowering parents had given Jenna that push to strive to succeed. The downside to such pressure was the inevitable anxiety. Jenna swallowed pills like they were going out of fashion, both the prescribed and non-prescribed varieties. It was a lethal concoction that had probably given her the stomach cramps. Until the doctors confirmed one way or the other, though, Jenna would continue to take her 'medicine'. "Where are they?"

On the wall above Jenna, the clock told her it was half nine. It was late on a Friday night. Jenna was supposed to be at home getting ready for a night on the town with her housemates, not lying on a gurney swearing at NHS staff to do their jobs faster. Still, she'd navigated the waiting room fast enough. Although, she suspected the nurses had simply substituted a padded chair in said waiting area for a lonely cubicle isolating her from everyone with only a flimsy curtain for concealment. Jenna was naked but for the gown she'd been asked to put on. Anyone could poke their head through the curtain and find themselves with a face full of her naughty bits.

The curtain whipped round and a woman in scrubs entered her cubicle. The doctor closed the curtain before standing over Jenna. She introduced herself as

Doctor Cheavers, holding a clipboard with Jenna's details. "So, Jenna, what seems to be the problem? You don't mind if I call you Jenna, do you?"

Even through the light blue mask Cheavers was wearing, Jenna could tell the woman was smiling. "Listen, if you stop these stomach cramps, you can call me anything you want." Jenna hoped she wasn't wasting the doctor's time, but with how much pain she was in, she really didn't care too much. Jenna needed the pain to stop. Even if she had to take more pills. "Please help; I'm in so much pain."

Cheavers took the time to examine Jenna's belly, prodding and poking various points. Does this hurt? How about this? What kind of pain? How would you rate the pain? They were all valid questions. Yes, yes, sharp stabbing pain and ten out of ten were her answers.

"Please, doctor, do something," Jenna pleaded. She wasn't expecting Cheavers to ask if she'd had sex recently? Jenna stared up at the doctor, her eyes wide. "I wouldn't say recently. Maybe four months ago? Why? You're not saying you think I'm pregnant, are you?" Jenna couldn't be pregnant. Until the pain had started a couple of hours earlier, there had been no signs. And if her one night thing with Phil had got her pregnant, she would have noticed by now, wouldn't she?

"Did he wear protection?" There was no judgement in Cheavers' eyes.

Jenna couldn't lie. That random night in a bar had ended as abruptly as it had started. Jenna had struck up a conversation with a bearded man at the bar. One thing had led to another, and before she knew it, he was taking her inside an abandoned factory that he told her he owned. Phil was a gentleman, making sure she was comfortable at every stage of the night. It was so exciting, being led down to a cellar full of exotic spiders, past these strange looking machines and into a small bedroom at the far end of the cellar. Jenna had been both scared and fascinated in equal measure going into the factory with Phil.

The first thing Jenna had noticed about Phil was how confident and good-looking he was. Confidence was a major turn-on for Jenna, she had to admit. In the bar, her friends had all commented on how fit he was, screaming toned muscles beneath his shirt. And Jenna had wanted to find out just how fit. And they were right, her friends. Phil was stacked. Chest muscles, abs, shoulder boulders and heavily muscled arms. She'd felt safe with Phil.

Not being an easy girl, Phil was only the second man she'd gone with since moving to the capital from Manchester to attend the London School of Economics on Houghton Street almost two years earlier. Even seeing the cellar full of spiders had only fascinated her; it had not appalled or scared her. Back in the bar, Phil had told her that he was a renowned arachnologist, so it wasn't a surprise to her to find his place awash with all things arachnid.

Sex for Jenna had always been a muted affair. The boys she laid down with were exactly that, boys. Most only cared about getting themselves off. Not Phil, though, no, he'd worked on her like a professional, making sure she enjoyed the experience as much as he had. For the first time in her life, Jenna had screamed in delight, biting his shoulder while Phil pounded her. Leaving Phil in the morning was hard, made more so by the fact he didn't seem to want to continue their union. That had hurt. Jenna had wanted to get to know him more.

"I'll take your silence to mean no, shall I?" Cheavers wrote something on the clipboard. "Well, there's something going on down there, Jenna. I'm just not sure, until I examine you."

Jenna almost gasped. She stopped herself by swallowing instead. "You mean?"

With a nod, Cheavers confirmed her worst fears. "I promise, I'll be gentle."

Looking away, pretending it wasn't happening, Jenna

spread her legs, allowing Cheavers access. It wasn't as painful as Jenna thought it might be. Having never been for a smear, she had no idea what to expect. Cheavers' fingers went inside, which was uncomfortable.

"Oh my God!" Cheavers whipped her fingers out and stared at Jenna. "We need to get you to the OR, now, Jenna. You're going to have a baby. These aren't cramps, honey; you're in labour."

Everything happened in a blur. Jenna kept arguing that she wasn't pregnant, she couldn't be. She'd only had sex with Phil four months earlier. How could she be pregnant? It made no sense. If she gave birth now, wouldn't it be wildly premature? Her arguments fell to the wayside. Cheavers and her nurses wheeled Jenna through to an operating room, where more medical personnel were waiting with all the instruments that Jenna recognised from TV programmes and films, mostly of the horror variety.

What was happening? It was Friday night; she was supposed to be downing shots of Sambuca, not being fussed over by strangers in scrubs and masks. It was too surreal to even comprehend. "Please, you don't understand, I can't be pregnant."

A sharp stabbing pain in her gut made Jenna double over on the table, her stomach on fire.

Cheavers took control, between her legs. "Right,

Jenna, when I say, I want you to push, okay?" Cheavers waited for Jenna to confirm with a nod. "Now, Jenna, push!"

Bar the pain, to Jenna it was like pushing on the loo when she had constipation, only different. It was all coming from and to a very different part of her body. She let Cheavers control the situation, pushing when ordered, and stopping when told to. After five pushing sessions, Jenna was sodden, her gown clinging to her skin. The only thought entering her mind was that she couldn't be pregnant.

"Right, Jenna, one final push, okay?" Cheavers was waiting with her hands poised.

Holding her breath, Jenna pushed so hard her face changed colour, turning slightly purple with the effort. The pain was overwhelming, making her want whatever was inside her out more than ever. It had to be over!

"Sweet Jesus!" Cheavers balked, taking a step back, her eyes wide with fear. The doctor spread her arms wide, stopping her nurses from going near Jenna.

Relieved that the pain had vanished, Jenna kept her eyes closed, smiling, until she opened them, the terrified expressions on the NHS nurses' faces making her sit up. "What is it?" None of them were holding her baby. There was no crying. Why was Cheavers holding her nurses back from tending to her baby? "Doctor? What is it? What's wrong?"

None of the emergency workers moved. But something was beneath her gown, something was between her legs. Jenna pulled her gown up.

She gasped at the grey sac sitting on her operating table covered in goo. It was long and silky, like it was coming out of her. Jenna pulled her gown up further, revealing her midriff, where she could see several lines of the silk extending from her vagina to the small sac. The sac was moving, shimmering. Something was alive inside it.

"No one move!" Cheavers strode to the back of the room, where a telephone was hanging on the wall. She picked up the receiver, dialling a number. "We need to start quarantine procedures in here, now. No one enters or leaves this OR, is that understood?"

The sac was the size of a watermelon, grey in colour and soft in appearance. Something like that should never have come out of Jenna's body. Desperate to get the lines of silk out of her, Jenna sat up and grabbed some. She reeled metres and metres of it out of her, stopping only when she had no more energy. Watching the sac quiver, the nurses stared open-mouthed. Jenna screamed.

2

FOUR MONTHS LATER

Helen Fisher clapped her son, Kyle, watching him in goal. Bless him, her son wasn't made for football, not in the slightest. He said he loved playing, but almost always grumbled about his teammates after a match. Grateful that he was in goal, rather than running up and down the green, hacking at the other boys' ankles, she gave him an exuberant wave. "Kyle! You're doing really well, honey." He was so embarrassed, Kyle gave her a slight wave back.

Why was she the only parent there? How could the other twenty-one kids' parents let them go to Clapham Common by themselves? They were only ten and eleven year-olds. Most of them probably only lived nearby, but still. With the world in the state it was in, Helen wasn't about to let Kyle out of her sight, not until she could trust him. Probably when he was eighteen, when a whole load of new fears would grip her. Thirty?

There was a boy running with the ball, a good-looking lad with dark hair that needed a good brush. Ben Ingham was in Kyle's class at school, a lovely boy by all accounts. Helen wished his parents were nicer; they were the most stuck-up snobs she had ever met. Everything was about image with them. Poor Ben's dad put Ben in Chelsea's youth team as an image thing. 'Look at my son everyone; he's going to play for Chelsea one day. Aren't we great!' Well, none of that was going to happen to Kyle. Nope, Helen was raising him the right way. He would learn the value of money; he wouldn't feel entitled. And rightly so. Helen and her husband, George, had worked hard for what they had.

"Come on, Billy! Take him down!" Kyle yelled in front of the goal.

The lad, Ingham, booted the ball at the makeshift goal, forcing her Kyle to dive for it. When the ball soared past Kyle into a bush, Helen clapped anyway. Encouraging Kyle in everything he did came naturally to her.

A man standing a little distance away sidestepped closer to her while she was clapping. Helen spied him out of the corner of her eye. Maybe he was the one other parent there? Ignoring him, Helen watched Kyle running over to the bush.

The man, a nice-looking black guy in a posh suit smiled. "He yours?"

"I got it!" Kyle carried on inside the bush.

"The goalie is, yeah," she replied, still watching Kyle. Her son got on his knees to fetch the ball, poking his head inside it. "Which one's yours?"

The man pointed to a boy on Kyle's side, who was busy kicking the jumper, beating the goal up. "That little psycho over there, Billy. I've warned him about his temper." He grinned.

"Mum!" Kyle shouted to Her, with his back to her, staring at his arm.

"Excuse me! Duty calls." Helen smiled before running across the green to her son's side. He was busy rubbing his arm.

"A spider bit me!"

"Let me look at that." Rubbing it, the bite looked painful. Helen had had quite a bit of experience with bites and stings. Every year, Kyle was either stung or bitten. When he was two, Kyle was stung by a hornet, the biggest bugger she'd ever seen. Her son had cried for hours. Helen tried finding the spider Kyle was pointing at, after showing her where it was. Helen saw a tiny little grey thing crawling away. It would do no one any good killing it, least of all Kyle, although there had been plenty of news coverage about a surge in spider bites of late. Thinking nothing of it, Helen paid full attention to her son instead.

Billy's dad came over asking what was wrong. Helen obliged in explaining the situation, before going back to Kyle's aid. "Kyle, honey, there's not a lot I can do except put some cream on it. Come on, I've got some Anthisan in the car." She took his hand and made to walk away. After a step, Kyle stopped, clutching at his chest.

"Mum!" Kyle started sweating, his breathing laboured. His little knees gave way.

Helen panicked, cradling her ten year-old son. "Kyle!"

Billy's dad's hand went into his suit jacket pocket for his mobile. "It might be anaphylactic shock." He took his mobile out and dialled. "I'm calling for an ambulance." He spoke animatedly, telling the caller on the other end that her son had been bitten by a spider. A small grey spider.

In her arms, Kyle's breath came in rasps. Helen helped him to focus on his breathing. There was a crowd gathered, Kyle's teammates and a smattering of adults. It felt like an age before an ambulance arrived.

While Kyle was lying on his back, being tended to by two paramedics, Helen was standing by her son's side, looking down at the medical staff trying to help him. She felt Billy's dad's arms on her shoulders. She was going out of her mind, different scenarios playing out in her mind. What if Kyle died? Would George forgive her for letting him play on the green? They were silly little thoughts that deserved no time.

The wind picked up all of a sudden. As did the noise.

"Mum! What's that?" Kyle's eyes were drooping.

A helicopter flew low overhead, like it was about to land on the common. Helen put her hands on her head, trying to keep her hair in place. The paramedics tending to Kyle were as confused as she. Helen looked to Billy's dad for an explanation; all she received in return was a shrug of his shoulders.

"What the hell?" The male paramedic looked down at Kyle and winked. "It'll be alright, kid. Stay with us. We need to keep you awake."

Several men in khaki uniforms came running up, carrying a gurney. Helen intercepted them, holding her hands out, trying to shield Kyle. "What's going on? Who are you?" One of them stopped and spoke to her while the rest went up to Kyle, pushing the paramedics out of the way. "What the hell are you doing? What are you doing to my son?" She went to grab the soldier in front of her. He told her that they were there to help Kyle. And to let them do their job, please. Although polite, there was no pleading in his eye; he was in charge.

When they placed Kyle on their gurney, Helen tried to get to Kyle, but the soldiers blocked her path. Her son was calling for her. He was frightened. "Kyle, I'm here, love." She wanted to go with him when soldiers picked up the gurney, carrying him off. "Kyle!"

Helen waited while they loaded her son into the helicopter. The soldiers remained steadfast in front of her until it was their time to leave, at which point she started after it. "Give me my son, you bastards! You can't do this!"

The soldier in charge was the last to get back on the helicopter. "He's safer with us. Let's go!" He shouted into his intercom. "I'm sorry, ma'am."

The helicopter took off with a noisy and windy farewell. Helen was helpless; her son was being abducted by men in British army uniforms. They appeared genuine in the clothing. What would the military want with her son? "Give me back my baby!" It was futile, she was certain, but the words were meant. She would bury anyone who touched her baby.

She watched as the helicopter rose further in the air before flying away with her Kyle. Tears of both frustration and anger rolled down her cheeks. With her hands, she wiped them away. "Kyle! I love you, baby." Her legs buckled beneath her, putting her on the grass.

Billy's dad took her hands when the sound of the

helicopter had faded away. "Come on! We're going to get your boy back." He helped Helen to her feet. "I'm Harvey Abbasi. I'm a human rights lawyer. The army can't do this. They can't just abduct your son like this without telling you where he's going."

Confusion clouded Helen's rational thought processes. "I don't understand what's...Where have they taken my Kyle?" She was pulled along by Harvey. "No! Wait! I need to speak with George. I need to tell George where our son is."

"That's the first thing we'll do when we get to my office, okay?" Harvey dragged her along the green again. "I got their helicopter number. I'll know where your son is by the end of the day, I promise."

3

Aaron Pike was bored of lying on the bunk, staring up at the white ceiling. It was so hard to get away from the white of the walls, ceiling, and floor. Even the white pyjamas he had been forced to put on when he arrived at the facility by helicopter were clinically white. The soldiers had forced him to give up his mobile and civilian clothing, before showering in some kind of delousing lotion. He imagined Colonel Trantor was the kind of man who liked white rooms. Or maybe he was in one of those torture rooms? Luckily, they'd not played white noise through speakers. Aaron was grateful for that at least.

With no mobile or watch, Aaron checked the clock on the wall: 09:36. He'd been locked in the room for a day and two nights, receiving three square meals in that time. The clock was the only thing giving him any bearings since being escorted to his home by armed guards, packing a suitcase in five minutes, and leaving a note for Lily, his wife. The guards didn't even let him phone her to tell him what was going on, just the note. Oh, how he wanted to hold Lily. He pulled himself upright and dangled his bare feet over the side of the bed. It was morning, about time to get some answers.

Jumping down from the top bunk, Aaron landed with a thud, groaning when his bad leg twinged, stretched, and padded over to the white door. "Alright, enough's enough. Let me out of here!" He banged on the door until the base of his fist hurt. There were no spy holes for him to look through. Checking the room again, the camera moved in his direction, having been trained on his bunk all night. "I know you can hear me. I want out of here." He waved both arms at the camera. "Time's wasting here geniuses. Those things are out there in case you hadn't noticed. Jackson and Hardcastle won't be the only ones. We could have up to two-hundred and fifty infectious spiders out there." He turned away from the door and limped back and forth inside his cell. "We need to be hunting these things down before we have an epidemic on our hands."

When he'd arrived almost thirty-six hours earlier and was locked in the room against his will, Aaron had banged on the door for hours, or what felt like hours at the time. There was no way he could sleep with the white lights above him, so what else did he have to do except protest his abduction? And he had been abducted, by some hard-arsed colonel and his automaton soldiers. Not one shred of individuality between them, the soldiers. They even looked alike; Aaron was sure he couldn't tell one apart from the rest. They were all burly, well-muscled, intimidating bastards. Colonel Trantor was the worst of the lot, though, the Alpha Male to rule them all.

His only interaction during his stay was when a female soldier entered carrying a first aid kit. Even she was heavy-set, with huge biceps and a steely stare. Contrary to her looks, she was tender when dressing his wounds, applying some sort of cream to the spider bites on his leg and chest. Getting undressed in front of her was uncomfortable, but Aaron was pleased to be getting treated. The bites hurt, where Zoe Hardcastle's babies had sucked on his fluids. Since the female soldier had left, Aaron had not spoken to anyone, including the soldiers who'd brought in his meals. Not one word from any of them.

The white door slid across with a hiss as some sort of gas was emitted from the doorframe. So far, Aaron's experience could only be described as futuristic. Bland, but futuristic. He stood back when a soldier clad in white uniform carrying an MP5 machinegun stepped inside and to the left. Another came in and stood to the right, leaving space for Colonel Trantor to meet him. "You! What's the big idea, colonel? You've had me cooped up in here for nearly two days."

Trantor refused to answer his questions. Instead, he smiled and stood to the side, pointing out to the corridor. "If you'll join me in the debriefing room, Mr. Pike, all will be explained."

He wasn't going to get any answers from the colonel. Aaron obliged, walking past the colonel and his subordinates. "You've got a thing for white, huh!" He made his way into the corridor, the colonel joining him.

"As I said, all will be explained." The colonel walked by his side.

There was no chit-chat, no apology. They walked to the end of the corridor, where Aaron noted they'd walked past at least ten cell doors on both sides, and his cell was halfway along the corridor, so there had to be twenty cells either side, forty in total. "What the hell is this place anyway?" He didn't expect a reply, when the colonel used his palm print on a panel to open an elevator door. Aaron stepped inside with his hosts, the soldiers carrying their guns.

The descent took mere seconds. The colonel stepped

out of the elevator first, waiting for Aaron to join him, leaving the soldiers on board. Following the colonel's lead, Aaron took in his white surroundings; everywhere was white, it seemed. They walked the length of the corridor to a white door, where Trantor used his palm for entry to a large debriefing room.

"Take a seat, please, Mr. Pike." Trantor indicated a row of seats.

The room had a high ceiling and enough seating for a hundred guests. Aaron chose a seat in the middle of the row and sat a few feet away from a man he recognised as one of the armed police who he'd entered Aldwych Station with only a couple of nights earlier. He tried to attract the officer's attention. Further down, on another row of seats, Aaron spotted Inspector Mike Newall, the police officer he'd first met at Philip Jackson's underground laboratory. "Inspector," he whispered.

No one reacted to his whispers; instead they all remained facing the front, eagerly awaiting the colonel's presentation, Aaron suspected. Taking the hint, he leaned back in his seat. Up front, Colonel Trantor went and stood behind the podium.

The colonel cleared his throat and spoke into the microphone that rang out with interference until he fiddled with the lead. "Good morning, ladies and gentlemen," the colonel started, switching on a projection unit overhead. "May I take this opportunity in expressing my sincerest apologies for keeping you waiting. We had an unexpected visitor arrive in our infirmary. It was touch and go for a few hours, but I'm glad to say the worst is over and our newest subject is alive and recovering. Anyway, moving along."

With ten souls watching on, Colonel Trantor used the projector to display a picture of a pretty young blonde girl. She couldn't have been any older than twenty. "Approximately four months ago, my superiors intercepted a quarantine message sent to Public Health England from the A and E department at Queen Mary Hospital. This twenty year-old economics student at the London School for Economics, Jenna Martin had been admitted for stomach pains. Upon examination, Doctor Eleanor Cheavers believed Miss Martin to be pregnant. After rushing her to the operating room, Doctor Cheavers sent the quarantine message." Trantor pressed the button on his controller, changing the picture to one of a brown sac sitting on an operating table. "This is what Miss Martin gave birth to that night. A perfectly formed, egg sac, containing Professor Philip Jackson's human-spider hybrid offspring."

Where there should have been murmuring, there was none. Everyone in the room had been abducted from the abandoned Aldwych Station, along with Aaron and Inspector Newall.

"I'm glad to say that we were able to save the offspring. It's currently gestating under observation in one of our top-security hatching cells, where the temperature is kept at optimum levels for its own protection and survival."

The poor girl had to be the student Jackson had spoken about in his video. He'd mentioned picking her up at a bar and fucking her, back before Jackson had turned into the widow, but after he'd been bitten. What a thing to go through! To give birth to a spider sac. It made him shudder, just thinking about it, Aaron raised his hand. "Colonel Trantor, is the girl alive?"

"I can confirm that Miss Martin is alive and well, yes, Mr. Pike," the colonel replied. "She has been invaluable in our research of these things we've named arachnoids. Through observation and testing, we now know a lot more about these arthropods, about their genetic structure and make-up. And now that we have the bodies of Professor Jackson and Zoe Hardcastle to autopsy, our understanding of this new species will grow."

They'd come up with the same name for them as Adele had, Arachnoids, which just a mixture of arachnid and humanoid. It wasn't rocket science, or anything, to mix two terms together. Aaron raised his hand again. "Forgive me, Colonel Trantor, but I believe Miss Martin was uninfected at the time of conception. Jackson was the infected party. Have there been any side-effects reported from Miss Martin?"

"We'll get to that soon enough, Mr. Pike." Colonel Trantor changed the photo to one of the dead body of Jackson lying on the ground of the derelict factory. "You'll have your chance to examine Miss Martin. I'm counting on you to help us understand how these things came to be. You'll be going through Professor Jackson's datafiles soon enough."

A door to the side of the room slid open. A soldier in white pyjamas went over to the Colonel and whispered in his ear. He thanked the soldier and regarded the delegation. "I'm afraid something has come up. Mr. Pike, will you join me down here, please. The rest of you, please remain seated while my colleague debriefs you on your roles and responsibilities here, at this facility. Mr. Pike, if you please?"

Without the need for more prompting, Aaron rose from his seat and made his way down to the podium, where Trantor met him.

"We need your opinion on an unexpected turn of events." Trantor took Aaron to the sliding door. "Put your palm against the panel, please."

4

Kyle Fisher awoke to silence. It was how he knew he was somewhere strange, silence being foreign to him in the mornings. Normally he would hear his mum and dad's voices in the distance, the sound of his mum getting breakfast ready. Or his mum would come in and gently rouse him. The white of the walls and ceiling made him shield his eyes. When he finally opened them properly, he was covered by a white sheet. "Mum?"

Instead of getting up, he curled into a ball beneath the sheet and put his thumb in his mouth. Where was his mum? Kyle tried to think back to the last thing he could remember, other than the nightmare he'd had about being trapped in a box with spiders. His heart started pounding when he recalled the big orange tarantula falling onto his chest, its fat hairy legs crawling up to his chin. And the thousands of spiders filtering into the box with him. He couldn't remember past screaming when the fat orange tarantula put its leg on his chin.

When a door on the other side of the room slid open with a hiss, Kyle curled up even tighter, his muscles tensed. It was like something from a Persil advert. A person wearing a white gown entered, wearing a hooded mask with a clear front. The face behind the visor was beautiful.

It was nothing like the mask he remembered. The very last memory he had was of a scarier mask staring down at him. A voice had said, "Stay with me, Kyle." His mum's shrill voice calling for him in his distant memory made him take his thumb out of his mouth. "You're not my mummy."

The figure in white came closer, holding something in her hand. Kyle uncurled himself and sat up, backing himself into a corner as the figure approached. The beautiful figure put her gloved hand out. His voice rose in pitch and volume, "I want my mummy!"

"Shh, it's okay, Kyle." The white clad figure's voice was soft and soothing. "I'm your friend. I'm here to help you."

Whoever she was, she had a different frame than his mum's, broader and shorter. Kyle tensed further, trying to make himself smaller. "Leave me alone," he shouted, closing his eyes, wishing he would wake up in his own bed. "I want my mummy!"

"Your mummy will be here soon, Kyle, I promise," she told him. "Before she gets here, though, I need to check you're okay. Can I do that, Kyle?" The figure in white reached his bed and sat on the edge. "My name is Chloe. I'm your friend, Kyle. I'm here to make sure you're healthy and safe."

After a lengthy pause, Kyle opened his eyes to find Chloe staring at him. "I don't like it! I don't like your mask. I don't like your voice." His pulse quickened as he closed his eyes tight again, praying to God that it was all a bad dream, like that one about the orange spider. "Go away! Go away!" He whispered under his breath, willing it.

"Shh, Kyle," the voice said. "The mask is for your protection, and mine. I'm not allowed to take it off, but you can see my face, can't you? Open your eyes, honey. See? I'm your friend. Please open your eyes. I want to talk to you, Kyle. You can trust me."

Kyle opened them to find Chloe smiling down at him. Up close, Kyle had never seen anyone so beautiful before; she had the most pointy features he'd ever seen, a pointy chin, nose and cheeks. And a smile that cut through him in an instant. Chloe had the most dazzling eyes, the bluest blue he'd ever seen, like he could jump inside them and take a swim. "When's my mummy getting here?"

"Soon, honey, very soon." Chloe picked up something in her hand. "But before she gets here, I need to get you ready, Kyle. Will you help me?" She went to touch Kyle, who flinched. "It's okay, I just need to check your vitals. Will you let me? This is what we call a stethoscope, Kyle. It lets me listen to your heart. You've seen one of these before, haven't you? A big boy like you must have had your heart checked with one of these?"

He couldn't resist her soft voice; it eased Kyle to the edge of his bed, where he let his legs dangle. Chloe asked him to unbutton his gown and lie on the bed. Kyle did as asked, lying on his back while Chloe listened to his heart. "Chloe, where am I?"

After Chloe had finished with her stethoscope, she smiled. "You're in hospital. It's a very special hospital set up for very special people, like you."

"Hospital?" Kyle scanned the room. "It's not like any hospital I've been in." There were no people, no machines. His room was plain and boring. Other than the bed he was lying on, there was nothing to look at, except the huge mirror on the wall next to the hissing door.

"Yeah? Well, like I said this is a special hospital for extra special patients." Chloe asked Kyle to get up, to sit next to her. "How much do you remember before waking up in here, honey? Do you remember fetching a ball from a bush?"

It came flooding back. Of course! He was playing football with his friends. Kyle was in goal when he had to fetch the stupid ball Ben Ingham belted through the goal. Stupid Ben Ingham! If it wasn't for him, he wouldn't have been bitten by a..."Spider. I was bitten by a small grey spider on my..." Kyle glanced down at his arm.

"You do remember? Well done, Kyle!" Chloe put her arm round his shoulder and squeezed. "You were bitten by a spider, that's right. You see, Kyle, we need to know what kind of spider it was before we can treat you properly. Can you remember what it looked like?"

Kyle stared up at Chloe's pretty face, wanting more than anything to remember. "It was grey, I remember that much. When it bit me, I yanked my arm out of the bush and it was stuck to my skin, so I flicked it off and it crawled away. All I can remember, really, is it was small and grey, with flecks of black on it. I'm sorry!" He was disappointed that Chloe wouldn't think it was enough. Kyle was delighted when Chloe ruffled his hair and told him he'd done well. "What's wrong with my arm?" Lifting it closer for inspection, Kyle noticed the tiny bite mark had strange lines protruding from them. "What are those?"

Leaning closer, Chloe examined his arm. "Oh, I wouldn't worry about those. It's where your body is fighting the infection, that's all. And you're doing so well." She rubbed his arm with her gloves. "So, we need to get you ready. I need to check your blood pressure, and later on this morning I need to wheel you down to the image scanning room. Would you like that? It'll be a little adventure for you."

"Are we getting ready to meet my mummy?" Kyle got up and plopped himself down on his host's lap. He wouldn't normally behave in such a childish way; since he couldn't hug his mum, he wanted to be close to Chloe. He hugged her tight, the fear fading when she put her arms around him. Kyle didn't want to give Chloe up.

5

"What's with all the white anyway?" Aaron stepped off the elevator, following Colonel Trantor along yet another corridor. "It's like a really bad Surf advert around here."

Colonel Trantor, whose white pyjamas carried markings on his lapels and insignia on his chest, stared ahead. "This facility is the most sterile environment on the planet, Mr. Pike. Every night the corridors and rooms are deloused using venting in the ceilings." He carried on walking while he talked. "A white surface is the easiest to clean, as I'm sure you're aware." He used his palm to open a door leading to another corridor.

Walking alongside Trantor, Aaron's bare feet were sore walking on the mat tiles. "So, level with me, colonel. What's the Ark? Is this place what I think it is?

Is it like some kind of underground bunker in case there's an apocalypse?"

With a smile, Trantor answered him. "It's not 'like' some kind of underground bunker, Mr. Pike, it is one. The Ark is a high security, state of the art facility where we store the DNA and genomes of every living creature on the planet. The bottom two levels are storage for the DNA, while levels six through thirteen will be home to the most important people in the country, and the top five will house politicians and their staff. It's the last hope of mankind." He stopped and opened a door leading to a separate room. "This is the future, but right now, while we can still live on the surface, it's a top secret research facility. Come inside, Mr. Pike, there's someone I want you to meet." Trantor waited for Aaron to step inside before closing the door.

When the door hissed shut, Aaron scanned the room, firstly noting the bank of monitors in front of a glass window. The monitors were sitting atop a desk. There were more screens and a bank of buttons at the rear. Stepping in front of the window, a member of the colonel's staff walked past. The staff member, who was wearing protective clothing walked over to a bed, where a young blonde girl was lying face-down. She couldn't have been any more than twenty years of age.

Colonel Trantor stood next to Aaron. "Meet Jenna

Martin. Twenty years old, an economics student at the LSE." He leaned across the desk and pushed a button. "Dr. Cheavers, what is that on Miss Martin's back?" He frowned, awaiting a response.

The woman sitting on the bed by Jenna Martin turned and stared at the window through her hooded visor. "I'm not sure, colonel. I was about to take a sample for a biopsy. It appears to be some kind of boil, or cyst. Shall I go ahead?"

Aaron glanced to his left, as Trantor nodded, leaned over, and held the intercom button. The colonel gave the green-light. In the isolation chamber, the doctor picked up a large needle and pierced the outer layer of the boil on the poor girl's spine, drawing out a vial of fluid before using an antiseptic wipe to cleanse it after. The boil was huge, about four inches in length and at least two inches wide; it was white and milky in colour. "What do you think it is?" Aaron asked the colonel, who shook his head.

"It could be a bed sore. Miss Martin's been comatose for almost four months, although she hasn't put on an ounce of fat in that time. She hasn't shown any sign of muscle wastage, or weakness in any way. It's like she's been in stasis this whole time."

There was something off about the whole set-up. Aaron had his suspicions the colonel wasn't being honest with him. "So, Jenna spent four months in a coma after giving birth to an egg sec? Is that why you couldn't find Jackson before we did? I mean, if you had her down here for months, I'm sure she'd have told you where she met Jackson?"

Turning to face Aaron, the colonel's expression was serious. "When we brought her here, we thought she was in shock. Naturally, after the trauma of birthing something like that, you'd expect nothing less, right? All the screaming and crying subsided a couple of days later. When Dr. Cheavers tried to illicit information from her, Miss Martin pulled the curtain down. She just lay on the bed, staring up at the ceiling. We tried everything to get her back." He turned to the window, staring at Jenna Martin lying on the bed, her head turned to face the colonel. A radio crackled to life on the bank of monitors.

"Colonel Trantor, you need to come to observation room four. It's the egg sac, sir."

Before Trantor could respond, Aaron jumped when Cheavers was launched from the bed onto the floor by Jenna Martin, who leapt from her mattress in her pyjamas. The young girl ran up to the window, her face contorted in anger. Stepping back, Aaron wouldn't have been surprised if she jumped through the window.

"Where's my baby?" Jenna hit her palms on the reinforced glass. "I want my baby!" She started sniffing at the air, moving to her left, then back to her right. "Where is he? Give me my baby!" Her fists hit the window, making it bow, and bounce back.

Trantor wasted no time in hitting the 'gas' button. "Dr. Cheavers, are you alright?"

Gas started billowing into the isolation room from vents in the ceiling. Aaron was speechless, watching Jenna turn her back on the glass, facing Cheavers, who was on her feet, her suit the only thing saving her from inhaling sleeping gas. Jenna ran at Cheavers, knocking her to the ground. The powerful young girl kept punching her doctor, one punch nearly breaking through the visor, until all power drained from her body, and she fell asleep on top of Cheavers. "Get Cheavers out of there, colonel, now."

Obliging, Trantor used his palm to open the door. He remained in the doorway, encouraging Cheavers to join him. The room was still misty from the gas when Trantor closed the door. He let out a sigh. "Sweet Jesus! I guess Miss Martin's finally up. Are you okay, Dr. Cheavers? Do you need to go to the infirmary?"

Her hands on her knees, Cheavers shook her head, catching her breath. After a few seconds, she stood up straight and took her hood and visor off, holding out her hand. "I'm Dr. Eleanor Cheavers. And you are?" She smiled at Aaron, waiting.

Doing the introductions, Trantor cut the getting to know you talk short. "You'll have plenty of time to catch each other up. We have an emergency next door." Trantor walked to the end of the room and opened another door, leading to observation room four, where he stood in front of another window of a far smaller box room. "Oh my!"

Visions of watching egg sacs open only a couple of nights earlier flashed through Aaron's mind, watching one open in the controlled environment. The grey sac wobbled. The four edges of the top uncurled, leaving a hole in the centre for the arachnoid to emerge from. It cried before showing itself, the familiar human baby cry, mixed with a hiss brought it all back for Aaron, who held his breath.

Black legs appeared first, before its basketball sized head and body climbed out of its home. The baby landed on the sterile floor with a thud, glancing around the room. It took the baby a matter of seconds to stop and stare at Aaron, Trantor and Cheavers. It cried.

"It's magnificent, isn't it?" Trantor stepped up to the glass, putting his hands on it. "Hey there, little one. Don't be scared." He went down onto his knees, encouraging it to meet him.

"You've got to be fucking kidding me!" Aaron couldn't believe it. "Colonel, we need to destroy these things, not make friends with them. For fuck's sake, it's not a baby." The colonel ignored him. "We need to be out there hunting these things down and destroying them, do you understand? Colonel? Jesus Christ! He's cooing over it now."

The baby arachnoid slowly sauntered over to the window, where it stared up at the colonel, its two lines of four eyes moving in all directions. After a couple of seconds, all eyes focused on the colonel. It cried before hissing at the glass, spraying it with a corrosive enzyme. The glass started steaming.

Had the colonel not been protected by the window, the enzyme would have melted his face. Trantor got to his feet, glaring down at the little monster. "That's gratitude for you. Don't worry, though, that glass is reinforced."

Aaron stepped back when cracks started to appear. "Um, colonel, we need to get out of here. That glass is going to go." He took hold of Cheavers' hand and pulled her back to the door. The cracks spread to the top and bottom.

"Code Red, observation room four. I repeat, Code Red." Trantor took a couple of steps back before the door opened behind Aaron and Cheavers. Three soldiers entered carrying flame units on their backs. Trantor opened the main door to the observation room, allowing the first soldier to enter.

The baby cried and hissed at the three soldiers in front of it, each pointing flame throwers at it. Before it attacked them, the soldiers engulfed it in a fiery ball for five seconds, letting it toast before they released the triggers. Baby Arachnoid screeched as it burnt to a crisp. When the flames were put out by one of the soldiers carrying an extinguisher, it was on its back, its eight charred legs curled inward.

"Damn it!" Trantor hit the wall with his fist. "That was our best asset."

"Well, I don't want to be the one to tell Jenna we torched her baby." Cheavers clutched at the marks on her neck, where the young woman had attacked her. "Although, I'm not sure she's through birthing sacs just yet."

Trantor turned to her. "What does that mean?"

"I'm not sure. It's just a theory." She put on her hood and visor. "Let me do the biopsy and I'll see if my theory holds water."

6

_____

Jenna was lying on the operating table, trying to catch her breath, the stabbing pain in her belly easing. Why weren't the nurses seeing to her baby? Why wasn't her doctor picking it up? Why were they staying back? The doctor was waving her staff away. With her hair stuck to her skin, sweat still dripping down her face, Jenna tried looking down, between her legs, but her gown was in the way.

So slowly, Jenna reached out with her hands. Why was she scared to look? When her fingers clutched at the bottom of her gown, they took their sweet time pulling it away. Jenna gasped at the object sitting between her legs, covered in gooey stuff from inside her. Her lips quivered when four flaps on the pulsing egg sac opened with a squelch.

The doctor ordered her nurses out of the operating room. All Jenna could do was sit as hundreds, no thousands of black

*and red spiders ran from the top of the egg sec, down its side
and onto the cold shiny metal operating table. She could hear
tiny voices calling for her. 'Mummy!' They were all calling
her Mummy.*

*Instead of helping her, the doctor and nurses left her in
the room with the spiders. They shut themselves outside,
locking the doors to the operating room. "Help! Help me!"
Jenna's voice was so small, she could barely hear it herself.
The doctor was watching her through the window. "Please,
help me!"*

*Hundreds of spiders ran along her legs, forcing Jenna
onto her back. Hundreds more joined them, covering her
torso, chest and shoulders, leaving only her face free.
"Mummy, we're hungry!" Jenna screamed at the first bite.
Once one had sucked on her, the rest joined it in sticking their
tiny fangs into her. Begging the doctor to help, Jenna couldn't
move while 'her babies' feasted on her.*

Jenna sat upright, her heart pounding at the visions
of all those spiders crawling over her skin. Her hair was
stuck to her face and her breathing was laboured. When
she glanced around the white room, she didn't recognise
the place. Where was she? Apart from the bed she was
sitting on, the room was devoid of furniture. A huge
window the length of the wall opposite gave her an
uneasy feeling. On the other side of the glass, a person
wearing a white protective suit was doing something.

"Hello?" Jenna whipped the sheet back and dangled her legs over the edge of the mattress.

Her back hurt, stung. Straightening up, Jenna felt behind her, trying to reach the small of her back. She gasped when she felt something big protruding from her spine. It was a good couple of inches long and maybe the same in width. It was bulbous. The only thing Jenna could think of was a boil, or cyst. She got to feet and tried to feel it more.

"Get back on your bed, or do you want me to gas you for the second time today?" The person on the other side of the glass had a tone of hatred in her voice. "I'll not tell you again."

"Please help me, what is this thing? It hurts. Please-"

"Jenna?" The woman in the protective suit, including hood and visor sounded surprised to see her. "Is that you? You're not trying to trick me, are you?"

Taking the pyjama top down past her shoulders, Jenna turned her back on the woman, peering over her shoulder. "What is that?" In the window's reflection, the thing on her back was milky white, not skin colour. "Whoever you are, please help me."

Hissing to life, a door next to the window slid across. The woman in the suit stepped inside and used her palm to close the door. "Jenna, it's me. It's...Dr. Cheavers."

Of course! Dr. Cheavers was the last person Jenna remembered talking to. All thoughts of the painful boil on her back evaporated when Cheavers stepped closer. A joy Jenna had not felt in years forced her to smile. "Dr, Cheavers, am I glad to see you!" She pulled her top up, and ran to her visitor's embrace, where her doctor gave her the warmest hug.

"I'm so glad to see you, finally." Cheavers rubbed her back.

Looking up at her taller doctor, Jenna was confused. "What do you mean finally? I was only talking to you about my stomach cramps just now." Taking in her strange environment, it suddenly dawned on her to ask, "Where are we anyway? Why am I wearing these pyjamas?" And studying her bare feet, she asked where her trainers were?

Cheavers put her arm round Jenna's shoulder and walked with her back to her bed. The emergency doctor sat next to her on the edge of the bed, turning to her so that they were face-to face. "How much do you remember about our talk, Jenna?"

She could recall waiting in the make-shift triage room for a doctor to see her. Then Jenna remembered Cheavers introducing herself. All those horrible questions, including had she been sexually active recently. Jenna put her hand over her mouth when visions of lying on the operating table flashed through her mind. The pain was excruciating. "Not a lot," she lied.

"Oh, Jenna, I wish I could tell you everything's going to be okay, I really do." Cheavers took a phone out of her suit and turned it for Jenna to see. "You had sex with Professor Philip Jackson, didn't you? This was the man you told me about."

Nodding, Jenna stared at the floor, ashamed. "It was only a one-time thing, I swear." When she checked for Cheavers' reaction, her doctor had her compassionate face on. "Why are you wearing that? What's with the visor?" She went to touch it, but Cheavers balked. "What the hell's going on, Dr. Cheavers? What is this place?"

"You're in quarantine." Cheavers got up and on her feet. "You've been infected with something, Jenna. You're in here until we can find a cure, okay? When you let Jackson in, he infected you, I'm sorry!" She got down on one knee in front of Jenna. With her gloved hand, she took Jenna's in hers. "I promise you I'm going to leave no stone unturned looking for a cure to this disease. You're my number one priority. You believe me, don't you?"

Thinking about it, apart from the painful cyst on her back, Jenna felt fine. Better than fine actually. If anything, Jenna felt powerful. "But I don't feel infected. Shouldn't I feel ill, or something? I'm as fit as a fiddle."

"I wish it were that simple," Cheavers countered. "It's not that kind of infection."

Two men in pyjamas stood on the other side of the window watching her and Cheavers. "Who are they?" Jenna pointed at them, suspicious. "Why aren't they wearing hoods like yours? Am I contagious then? Is that it?" The full horror of her situation was starting to hit home when Cheavers sat back down on her bed.

"The taller man is Colonel Nathan Trantor, the caretaker of this facility. He's in charge, Jenna. And the gentleman next to him is Aaron Pike, an entomologist looking into this infection." Cheavers waved at her boss.

"It's so good to finally meet you, Jenna. It's great to see you up and about." The colonel's voice boomed through the intercom speakers built in to the walls of Jenna's isolation room.

It was the second time Jenna had heard the word 'finally' in as many sentences. Something wasn't sitting right in her gut. When she glanced across at Cheavers, her doctor was signalling to the colonel to back off. "What the hell's going on here anyway? How long have I been here, Colonel Trantor? And don't lie to me. One minute I'm in the operating room in hospital, the next I'm waking up in a strange place, surrounded by strangers in protective suits." She got up and walked over to the window. Trantor was being cagey.

"You've been here for a couple of days, tops." The colonel wasn't very convincing.

The other man in white pyjamas and bare feet stepped closer to the glass. "Four months, Jenna. I know this will come as a shock to you, but you've been in this facility for four months, since you gave birth to-" The colonel yanked on the other man's shoulder.

Another vision flashed through Jenna's mind: the pain that wracked her belly was succeeded by the terror of pulling back her gown to find...She gave birth to something...It wasn't a baby. And how she'd screamed. And screamed. Jenna's knees gave out, putting her on the floor. Cheavers went to her aid, as Jenna glanced up at the two men. "I've been here for four months? But I don't remember this place. It feels like I was in the hospital only yesterday. What have I been doing? And what came out of me? That thing wasn't my baby."

The colonel wouldn't look at her. "Dr. Cheavers, I need to speak with you in private, please." He glanced down at Jenna. "You'll get your answers, Jenna, I promise. I'll let the good doctor fill you in. Aaron, you and Dr. Cheavers will join me in examination room six. Until next time, Jenna, please try and relax. If you want to watch some TV, there's a remote by your bed. When you press the red button, it comes out of the ceiling. And for what it's worth, I am sorry you've found yourself in this situation."

Jenna sobbed as Cheavers left her room via the hissing door. No one was telling her anything. What had she given birth to? And what had she been doing here for four months? Why couldn't she remember anything?

7

Aaron got on board the elevator last, joining the colonel and Dr. Cheavers. The doors closed and Trantor turned to his resident doctor. Getting in there first, Aaron asked Cheavers what was going on with Jenna? Where she'd been for the past four months? The colonel gave Aaron a look that told him to shut up, the colonel was the one asking the questions.

Waiting, Trantor glared at Cheavers, who was still wearing her hood and visor. "And?"

"And what?" Cheavers stared straight ahead. "I don't have any answers yet. Maybe when my assistant comes back to me with the results of the biopsy, I'll know more. If I gave you an answer now, it would only be a guess."

"So, give me your best guess then." Trantor put his palm on the control panel, stopping the elevator between floors. "We're not moving until you tell me what you think you know."

Leaning against the rear wall with his arms crossed, Aaron listened while Cheavers explained how she believed Jenna's 'baby' had a psychic connection to Jenna. And about how Jenna being comatose during its incubation period might explain why she burst out of her coma when the egg sac opened, releasing Jenna's 'baby'. When Cheavers highlighted Jenna's miraculous recovery shortly after the Arachnoid was burnt to death, Aaron believed the doctor's theory. "Thinking about it, Zoe Hardcastle could communicate with her babies."

Starting the lift again, it took mere seconds for the elevator to reach its destination. They exited the lift two floors lower than they'd boarded. Aaron walked alongside Cheavers and behind Trantor. "Where are you taking us now, colonel?"

In answer to Aaron's question, Trantor opened a door on his left. It hissed open. Following Trantor, Aaron and Cheavers had to stop and stare through the window at two horribly disfigured black and red bodies laying side by side on matching operating tables. There were three members of Trantor's protected staff working on the corpses of Jackson and Zoe Hardcastle. Unsettled, Aaron almost jumped when one of the remaining legs on Zoe's body moved, like it was still alive.

"Relax, Mr. Pike, it's a spasm. They're both very dead, I assure you." Trantor smiled to himself at Aaron's ignorance of dead bodies and how they twitched after lights out. "I need you in there, working on those bodies, okay? I need to know what they are, how they work, how they communicate, do you understand?"

Confused, Aaron watched on the screen above him as one of the doctors inside the examination room used a scalpel to make an incision along Jackson's sternum. He wasn't green when it came to investigating biology; he'd dissected enough insects in his time, but watching the incision being made on the Arachnoid made Aaron queasy. "You want me in there? With them?" Trantor nodded. "I don't even get why I'm here in the first place, colonel. I'm not a doctor, I'm nothing. I'm just a lowly entomologist. All I want to do is go home and hug my wife, okay?"

Colonel Trantor watched the autopsy with Aaron. "Don't be so hard on yourself. You found Jackson when we couldn't, and believe me, we tried locating him. In fact, I'd put your investigative skills right up there, Mr. Pike." He glanced over at Aaron and smiled. "So, please do me a favour and help me out here, yes? I know it's hard being away from Lily."

"At least let me call her, please." He waited while the colonel collected a protective suit from the far wall of the room. Trantor walked back and handed it to Aaron. "Colonel, please let me speak with her." Aaron started putting the protective clothing on.

"Maybe tomorrow, Mr. Pike." The colonel was too vague. "Let me spell this out to you the best way I know how, okay? We're on the cusp of a possible pandemic here. You said yourself we have over two hundred venomous spiders out there, not to mention two arachnoids unaccounted for. If even a handful of these mutated spiders are infectious, there's no telling how many civilians might fall victim to this disease. Hell, we don't know how long these spiders have been missing for. We could already have a dozen infected civilians out there, slowly turning into these things, do you understand?" Trantor glared at him. "Now, please, put the greater good above your personal life for a second, would you? I need you in there working on this, okay? We need to know how these Arachnoids operate. I'll tell you what: you get me all the information I need, I'll let you video conference Lily, how's that?"

The colonel held all the cards. Aaron only had 613 clearance, meaning he only had access to floors six through thirteen. If he wanted out of the underground facility, he would need level one clearance that only a handful of officers had. As far as Aaron knew, the colonel was the only person with 115 clearance. "Well, it looks like I don't have a choice, doesn't it!" Aaron put the hooded visor over his head, the enclosed nature making him claustrophobic. He took a couple of deep breaths.

"Colonel Trantor, that was my assistant calling."

Aaron turned to find Cheavers putting a mobile phone in her pocket. It was a small phone, probably only an internal one used for communicating between floors, but Aaron had to find out. He continued putting his clothing on, listening to the colonel and Cheavers.

"Go on! I'm all ears, Dr. Cheavers." Trantor started helping Aaron with the hood, flattening it down.

Cheavers, still in her protective bubble sighed. "We've analysed the fluid taken from Jenna's back." She paused for reflection, until the colonel told her to get on with it. "It's amniotic fluid, colonel."

In an instant, Aaron stopped fussing with his suit. The two words used by Cheavers should never have come out of her mouth. He noticed the colonel stopped helping him with his suit. There was a stunned silence between the three of them.

It was the colonel who broke the quiet. "You mean... Jenna's carrying an egg sac on her back? Is that what you're telling me?" His eyes kept moving, left then right.

With a grave nod, Cheavers managed an "Uh-huh!" She fetched the vial from inside her suit and held it up to the light in the ceiling. "An unfertilised egg at that.

Who knows how big it will eventually grow to? Or how many offspring she'll be able to carry in it." The doctor stared at the floor, her face grave for the poor girl.

"But why?" The colonel clicked his fingers, waking Cheavers up. "She's not carrying any more of Jackson's children, is she? Why would an egg sac start growing on her back? It doesn't make sense. Unless-"

Having an idea of why, Aaron interrupted. "Unless she is being changed for future purposes. We know she's already produced one offspring. Maybe her body is adapting for future growth? She's fertile; she'll grow more. Her body's adapting to these changes." He wished he had never found Jackson or had any clue about the so-called Arachnoids. "That poor girl. How are we going to tell her about this?"

"That's up to you and Dr. Cheavers." The colonel's attention was drawn to the intercom on his pyjamas. "Go ahead, this is Colonel Trantor."

While the colonel was busy talking over the intercom, Aaron studied Cheavers for any sign of compassion. He walked over to her. "So, how are we going to broach the subject to Jenna? We can't tell her she's growing an egg on her spine, can we? Is there any chance we can drain it? Do you think that might help?"

As Cheavers was about to speak, Colonel Trantor hushed them both and pushed a button on the bank of monitors as a television descended out of the ceiling. Within thirty seconds, a bald man in his sixties with a grizzled and haggard face glared back at them, wearing his green army suit, complete with medals and insignia. "Brigadier Winston, welcome!" Trantor stood up straight and tall, saluting the angry man on screen. "What can I do for you this morning?"

The brigadier leaned closer. "You can start by doing your job, Trantor. Tell me why I'm getting messages from a human rights lawyer swearing blind he's going to be putting a woman named Helen Fisher on the evening news unless we take her to her son, Kyle. Tell me why, Trantor."

Lost for words, the colonel looked to Aaron for help. "I don't know, sir. We used unmarked helicopters. Or at least I think we did."

Even to Aaron, the colonel sounded weak. "Brigadier Winston, hi! I'm Aaron Pike. I've been brought in to help bring this situation to an end. Might I suggest we bring Mrs Fisher in? There's only so much your staff here can do to keep him calm and sedate. Having Klyle's mum here might help. It's just a suggestion, sir. It's your choice, of course."

"I concur with Mr. Pike, sir," Cheavers added. "She will be invaluable in helping us study Kyle's condition."

Cheavers stood back, letting Aaron and Trantor take point.

The brigadier sat back with a sigh. "Very well, bring her in. Trantor, we need to keep this quiet, okay? At least until we know what we're dealing with. Have word sent out to your field teams to keep it on the down low, is that clear? We don't need a panic on our hands. Oh, and Mr. Pike, is it? We're relying on you to come through for us. We need to know what these things are, okay? Don't disappoint me." He hung off, leaving the monitor blank.

As soon as Trantor was free to talk normally, he ordered Aaron into the examination room, where Aaron joined the two doctors conducting the autopsies. It freaked him out every time a leg twitched. "Right, let's see what we're dealing with."

8

Harvey Abbasi placed the phone receiver back on its cradle. "It's confirmed. They'll be here in fifteen minutes to pick you up, okay?" He stood up behind his big wide desk.

Helen was so relieved. She turned and gave her husband, George the longest, warmest hug before thanking Harvey for his help. They were going to see their boy again. "Let's go outside and wait for them, honey." She went to hold her husband's hand. She didn't like the way Harvey cleared his throat. "What is it, Harvey?"

The human rights lawyer in his expensive grey suit frowned an apology. "I'm so sorry, but they only agreed to you going, Helen. They wouldn't budge on George joining you. I tried everything I could to convince them. I threatened them as far as I could."

Disappointed, Helen nodded her understanding. "I see." She looked up at George's sad face, shaking her head. "I'll sort it when I'm there, darling, I promise." She could tell her husband wasn't so sure. He accepted it and carried Helen's packed bag outside Harvey's office building. When she stepped outside it was almost three in the afternoon. Still excited about seeing Kyle, Helen spent the remaining ten minutes hugging George.

The car arrived and Helen got in the rear passenger seat, where she smiled at George for the last time. She didn't want to leave him. After a minute of saying goodbye the soldier driving ordered her to close the door.

Before the soldier drove Helen away, he turned to her in his seat, handing her a blindfold. "Are you serious? You want me to wear this?" The soldier, a young guy in his early twenties explained that if she didn't comply with the rules, she should get out. "Alright fine." Putting the blindfold on, she realised how serious the army were about security. Where the hell were they taking her?

With the blindfold on, Helen was disoriented, forever rolling with the car, leaning to the left or right with every turning. Without access to her watch or mobile, she was unable to gauge how long the car journey had taken before they slowed to a stop at a private airport. Briefly allowed to take the blindfold off, Helen couldn't identify the place; there were no signs with names of places. She was marched straight from the car to a waiting chopper, where she was strapped in by the same soldier who'd driven the car. Helen was asked to put the blindfold back on before take-off. She argued that she wasn't near any windows. It didn't matter; she was forced to obey.

The flight could have taken an hour or five for all Helen could make out. It was a loud, bumpy and frightening journey, the turbulence enough to make her belly lurch on several occasions. "Is it going to be much longer?" She asked finally, receiving no reply.

Tired and frustrated, Helen relaxed a little when their chopper began its descent. On the ground, the helicopter's blades slowing down, her soldier took the blindfold off and asked her to follow him. She obliged, taking in the surroundings as she exited the chopper. They had to be on the roof of a large building. There was nothing for miles, nothing but fields as far as the eye could see. "Where are we?" Her question remained unanswered.

Reaching an emergency exit door, Helen followed the driver inside, where he invited her into an elevator.

The doors shut, but the lift stayed where it was. The soldier standing by her side, turned to her and ordered her to strip. Helen smiled. "Excuse me?"

"If you want to see your son, you need to remove your clothing," he explained. "You need to be vetted, cleansed and examined before you enter the Ark. Please remove your clothing."

Helen paused for a few seconds, her mind trying to understand why her hands were pulling her T shirt over her head. She took her trainers and jeans off. Standing in knickers and a bra, Helen checked the soldier's reaction, shrugging. "Happy now?"

"And the rest, please, Mrs Fisher." The soldier picked up her clothes while Helen took off her bra and handed it to him.

Mumbling about being forced to strip, Helen took off her knickers and stood next to the soldier, waiting for the lift to start. Her arm went to automatically covering her breasts and her free hand went between her legs. The lift started and stopped very quickly, meaning they'd probably only gone down three or four stories.

It almost hurt her eyes when the elevator door opened. Everything was white, from the floor, walls, and ceiling to the pyjamas the soldiers were wearing. In stark contrast to their clothing, were the guns they were carrying. Helen followed two new soldiers, both female, who took her clothes from her driver. Feeling exposed in front of so many eyes, Helen followed her escorts to what appeared to be a shower room. "You want me in there?"

"Five minutes, Mrs Fisher," one soldier replied. "You have fives minutes to wash and delouse yourself, okay? You'll find a bottle in each shower. Oh, and do yourself a favour: use the delousing agent all over. Don't be shy with it."

In under five minutes Helen had showered and dried herself using a towel given by the soldiers. The towel was taken away from her. "Um, where are my clothes, please?"

"That comes later, Mrs Fisher." The tall slender soldier beckoned Helen to follow her along a corridor, where she passed two more soldiers, both of whom ignored her. Relieved, she followed the soldier until they were in an examination room, complete with a patient bed with stirrups and varying shiny silver implements. When ordered into the chair, Helen balked, staring at the sharp instruments. "Is this really necessary?"

"If you want to see your son, it is, yes." The soldier helped Helen into the chair, tying her legs into the stirrups. "Don't be thinking you're special, or anything, We've all gone through this process. Just lie back and relax. The doctor will be with you shortly."

How could she lie back and relax? She was tied to a chair in a blindingly white room, being watched by soldiers with guns wearing pyjamas and nothing on their feet. If she had clothes on, she might have relaxed a bit.

"Mrs Fisher, I'm Dr. Cheavers," a woman in pyjamas entered, sitting herself down on a chair in front of Helen. "I'm pleased to meet you. Kyle's been asking after you. He's going to be so pleased you're here." The doctor picked up a syringe.

How could the woman be so familiar with her? "Yeah, can you explain to me why I'm tied to this bloody chair, please? I had a smear test last year; I wasn't planning on having another one for a few years, so-"

"This is the most sterile environment on the planet, Mrs Fisher. Every person in this facility has to undergo a battery of testing before they're allowed in. And since we're putting you through faster than normal, I'd appreciate it if you would just lie back and breathe normally. It'll be over before you know it, I promise."

The woman called Cheavers took four vials of Helen's blood, along with a smear test and a blood pressure reading while telling her how lovely Kyle was. Helen gritted her teeth and tried smiling at the right times.

Fifteen minutes of discomfort later, Cheavers untied

the leg restraints and let Helen get out of the chair. A soldier entered carrying some kind of suit with a hood and visor. The doctor explained to her that when she entered the observation room, she was not allowed to take the hood off, no matter how much Kyle wanted her to. The doctor informed Helen that if she did take off the hood, she wouldn't be put in the same room as her son. No, she would be separated from him until the all-clear was given. Helen nodded her understanding while changing into the protective suit. It was great to be wearing clothing again, she had to admit.

Wearing the thick suit on the way down in the lift was stuffy and hot. Helen wanted to take off the hood, but resisted, the thought of seeing Kyle exciting her. Stepping off the elevator, Helen followed the doctor to a room with a window and desk loaded with monitors. A smile formed when she saw her only child sitting on a bed at the rear of the room. Kyle didn't see her because he was too busy talking to or playing with someone else in a white protective suit. "Kyle!" She went up to the glass and tapped on it with her gloved hand. "Kyle, it's mummy!"

It took her little boy a few seconds to register her voice. When he finally recognised her, Kyle launched himself from his bed, racing to the window. "Mummy! You're here!" His face lit up when she squatted down to his level, the only thing separating them was a thick shield of glass. "Why are you wearing those funny clothes, mummy? You look just like Chloe."

Getting up, Helen turned to Cheavers. "Chloe?" When the doctor pointed into the room, Helen followed her finger to the figure inside the room with Kyle. The member of staff in the suit gave her a little wave as she walked toward the window. When the pretty young girl in the suit reached the glass, she put her hand on Kyle's shoulder. Helen's smile faded, as she turned back to Cheavers. "Can I get in there, please. I want to hug my son."

The doctor walked with Helen to the door. "Remember what I said, Mrs Fisher. If you or Kyle take your hood off, you'll be quarantined separately. Neither one of you will be happy in isolation, will you?" Cheavers placed her palm on the panel. "Tomorrow we'll get your security clearance sorted. Then you'll be able to open doors yourself."

The door hissed and opened, allowing Helen access to her son's room. She stepped inside as the door closed directly behind her. As soon as she got inside, Kyle ran over to her and gave her the biggest hug. Helen ruffled his hair before squatting and staring into his beautiful blue eyes. "I've missed you so much, Kyle. Daddy wishes he could be here. We'll try and get him to visit us, okay?"

When she looked up, Chloe was watching them with a silly smile. "Um, Chloe, is it?" The young woman nodded. "Would you give us a minute? I would like to be with Kyle alone for a while, please."

Her son pulled away from the embrace. "This is Chloe, Mummy. Chloe's my friend. Isn't she beautiful?" He got off his knees and onto his feet, grabbing Helen's hands. "Come on over to my bed, mummy! You're going to love Chloe; she's so funny."

Ignoring Helen's plea, Chloe followed them to the bed. Helen sat one side of Kyle and Chloe sat the other. She so badly wanted to yell at the woman to leave them alone. Not that it would have done her much good, as Kyle seemed smitten with his new friend. She listened to Kyle talking, noticing the marks on Kyle's arm. "Let me take a look at your bite, will you?" Helen took hold of her son's arm, studying the tiny veins spreading from the two puncture wounds. "Um, Chloe, what are these?"

The young woman shrugged inside her suit. "You'll need to discuss Kyle's condition with Dr. Cheavers, I'm afraid, Mrs Fisher. I don't have clearance." Chloe picked up the remote control from the bed sheets and pressed the standby button, as a TV appeared from the ceiling. "Find something to watch while your mummy and I talk to Dr. Cheavers, okay?"

Leaving Kyle alone, Helen managed to grab Chloe as

they reached the door. "Just level with me here, will you? What's going on? Why are we all here, huh? Kyle was only bitten by a spider. What's with all this cloak and dagger stuff?" She didn't give Chloe room to move.

"Look, it wasn't just a spider bite, okay? Your gorgeous son's infected with some sort of virus." Chloe tried to get past her to open the door. "Please, Mrs Fisher, let's go and talk to Dr. Cheavers. She'll answer all your questions. Or the ones she can at least."

9

TEN DAYS LATER

Kyle kicked the ball out to mid field, where one of his teammates managed to get it under control. In goal again. He might have been the tallest boy in his year, but he could do so much better up front. Every time one of his team took possession, they would lose it, leading the other team's striker heading back to Kyle. Something was weird, though. Why were they playing in the dark? The only light was coming from the huge moon above them. It was the biggest moon Kyle had ever seen, almost a huge lightbulb in the sky.

As Kyle stared up at the huge glowing orb, the ball went whizzing past him. Brought back to reality with a groan, Kyle turned to fetch the football. "I got it!" When he went past the jumpers for goalposts, there was a big wooden building in front of him. He would swear blind it wasn't there before. Looking for backup, Kyle glanced over his shoulder at his team.

There was no one there. Kyle wasn't on the green anymore. Looking down at the ground, he was walking on mud and stones. He swallowed. The huge barn in front of him had its doors open. It was a big black hole, which resembled a mouth. Wait! There was light flickering inside it. The two windows on the mezzanine level made the barn resemble a face, the doors for a mouth and windows as eyes. Why was he still walking towards it?

Taking in the environment, it appeared he was on some sort of farm. There were other buildings around, one looked like a farmhouse, others were outhouses. How had he ended up here? "Hello?" He continued in the direction of the barn. "Is anybody home?"

When he reached the doors, Kyle hid for a few seconds, before peeking inside. It was an empty barn with straw on the floor. Apart from the straw, it appeared deserted. "Hello?" His voice low, quiet, Kyle stepped inside. "I just want my ball back."

Something scurried up on the mezzanine level. It was big by the sound of it, human size. Kyle's little heart was beating so fast. He couldn't see the ball anywhere. The thing upstairs scuttled about. What was it? "Hello? I'm a friend." Why were his hands and feet on the ladder leading upstairs? And why was he climbing?

Poking his head above the last step, Kyle could not see anything, or anyone. He climbed all the way up and stood on the landing. The only objects on the floor were hay bales, oblong in shape, but big enough to hide a person. "Hello?"

Something black emerged from behind the bale. Kyle should be terrified of its shape, its six legs and two arms complete with hands. Its face was shiny and black, its fangs sharp and long. Why wasn't he scared? Kyle said nothing; he kept stepping forward, each step making the visitor step in his direction.

It was big, his height but with a longer body. Kyle was standing in front of it, whatever it was. Its hands reached out for him, until its palms touched his cheeks. Instead of speaking, it made a crying sound. It was a youngster, like him. Its touch soft and gentle, Kyle moved closer, putting his arms round its face, feeling its warmth to his touch.

With a start, Kyle sat up, drenched in sweat. He yanked the sheet away from him and got to his feet. The room was dark until a couple of seconds after his feet touched the tiled floor, when the lights flickered to life. "Mum! Chloe!" It was the fourth night in a row Kyle had dreamed of that thing in the barn. He only wished he had a name for it.

Checking his arm, Kyle noted how much farther the grey veins had spread, from his wrist, all the way along, to his shoulder. They'd grown in width as well as length, meaning his arm was a mix of grey and flesh colour. No one had explained anything to him, other than he'd been infected by the spider bite. Infected by what, Kyle had no idea. Even his mum couldn't tell him. Something else had happened. As well as the veins growing, his body was changing with it. He was growing muscle like nothing before. Kyle followed famous people on Instagram, he knew that girls loved pecs and abs. He had abs coming through, without even training. Kyle had not started some new diet; he'd not started a new exercise regime. In fact, being locked away inside his cell, Kyle was getting less exercise than ever before.

"Kyle, is everything okay?" Chloe walked through the hissing doorway and stopped in front of him. When she got close, she gasped inside her hood, putting her hand to the glass of her visor. "Dr. Cheavers! We need you down here right away."

The fear in Chloe's voice made Kyle take a couple of steps back. What was she so afraid of? Why was Chloe looking at him like he was a monster? He kept taking steps back until Chloe reached out for him, at which point he ran for the bathroom door. Kyle managed to get inside before Chloe could reach him. With the door closed, Kyle went and sat on the lavatory seat, his heartrate through the roof. "Leave me alone!" The words he'd uttered were his own, but the voice was not. "What the hell?" His voice was deeper, stronger, more mature.

Getting to his feet, Kyle approached the sink with the room's only mirror. It was his turn to gasp when he saw his reflection. It wasn't him; it was some older boy's face staring back at him. His heart rate spiked at the sight. It had to be him, didn't it? Kyle tested the reflection by performing a couple of moves, convinced it was him when the arm moved the same way twice. It was him, but it wasn't. How could the stranger staring back be him? "Mum! I'm scared!" His legs gave out from beneath him, as the door opened.

"Kyle!" Chloe ran over to him and took him into a hug on the floor. She gently rocked him back and forth until he was lying on her lap with his thumb in his mouth. "Dr. Cheavers will be here any minute now, sweetie. Hold on. Help's on its way. She'll be able to give us answers, I know she will."

"Who am I?" Kyle had to take his thumb out to speak.

"You're still Kyle Fisher," Chloe reassured him. "You might look different in the mirror, but you're still my little Kyle, okay? You'll always be my little Kyle, no matter how fast you grow." She carried on rocking him.

Someone appeared at the window. Kyle couldn't make out who it was until he lifted his head and took a closer inspection. Dr. Cheavers' gasp through the intercom was almost as big as his own when he'd seen his reflection. "What's wrong with me, Dr. Cheavers? I just want to go home. I just want to play footy with my friends."

Stepping through the cleansing mist in the doorway, Cheavers appeared wearing her hood and visor. "I wish I knew what was happening to you, Kyle, I really do. Gosh, you look, what fifteen? Let's get you in the imaging chamber, shall we? Let's see what's going on inside you." She remained by the door.

Obeying, Kyle followed Dr. Cheavers and Chloe to the elevator, where they went up one floor to the imaging chamber. After eleven or twelve days (that felt like months) Kyle had a map in his head of the whole facility, at least the parts he'd visited. He assumed the position, letting Chloe undress him. Once his pyjama top was off, Chloe pulled down his trousers. "What the-" He'd heard about the changes boys go through, puberty. "Should that look like that? And what about all that hair? Why is it hairy?"

Cheavers took Kyle's clothing from Chloe, chuckling. "In all honesty, Kyle, that's normal. It's the most normal thing about you." She got down on one knee, taking his arm in her hands. "I see it's spread even more. How are you feeling? I mean, apart from scared because of all this?" Cheavers stared up at him expectantly.

Thinking about the question, there could only be one response. "Great! Apart from this little surprise I feel fantastic. I'm so strong, I could take on the whole world. I thought you said I was sick? I don't feel sick. If anything, I'm better than before."

"Uh-huh!" Cheavers patted the bed of the chamber. "You know the drill by now, Kyle. Lie back, close your eyes and this will be over before you know it.

Lying with his arms by his side, Kyle didn't mind being naked in front of Chloe or Dr. Cheavers anymore. After the first couple of scans, it was like water off a duck's back as far as he was concerned. And having a man's bits, rather than a boy's bits made it less embarrassing. The machine flashed a few times, making a whirring noise. According to Dr. Cheavers, it was a huge X-ray machine that allowed her to study him from the inside. He'd seen a few images of his body a couple of times; it was hard to believe he was made up of all those squishy organs.

"That's it, Kyle, you can get dressed now." Cheavers handed him his pyjamas.

"Can't I wear something different, Doctor? And I'm going to need bigger jim-jams now, aren't I? These were so tight on me this morning, I nearly fainted." Instead of putting the pyjamas on, Kyle handed them back to Chloe and sat on the bed of the scanner. "And how long am I going to be here for? You haven't even told me what I've been infected with yet."

Cheavers asked for some bigger pyjamas into her radio, before regarding him. "I know how frustrating this must be for you, Kyle. I'd hate being cooped up here every bit as much as you do, but you have to trust me. The doctors here are doing all they can to give you the answers you deserve. All I can say is if there's a cure out there, we'll find it. I promise you that you're my top priority, okay?"

Unable to argue, disappointed, Kyle folded his arms and waited for the soldier to arrive with his new, bigger pyjamas. He almost sniggered at the shocked expression on the man's face when he saw him. After getting dressed, Kyle walked with Chloe back to the lift and his room. In the elevator, he noticed he was taller than Chloe. She was the most beautiful woman he'd ever met.

10

"Let me out of here! It's ten o'clock already!" Helen banged on the door of her room, which was more a cell than her place of rest. On her second day at the facility, she'd been given a 67 clearance (meaning she had access to only floors six and seven), but they insisted on locking her up at night, so she had to wait to be let out the following morning. "Breakfast is almost over, you arseholes. Let me out! I want to see my son!"

Pacing back and forth, all Helen wanted to do was be there for her poorly Kyle. For the past ten days she'd watched those veins growing along his arm, getting longer and fatter. Before she'd gone back to her room last night, Helen had taken a look at his arm: it was almost half covered in grey veins with black flecks. It had not spread further, which was a good sign, Cheavers had told her. "I swear if you don't open this door in the next five seconds, I'm going to kick the bastard down, do you hear me?"

The door hissed open, the familiar spray preceded two soldiers entering. Standing up straight, Helen fixed her pyjama top and walked into the corridor with her chin up. She then followed the soldiers to the lift, where instead of going up to Kyle on floor six, the soldier pushed the button to go to floor five. "I don't have clearance for floor five, you know."

"No, but we do, and so does Dr. Cheavers." One soldier replied with a sneer.

They were all bad tempered, the soldiers, Helen had noticed. Who was she to argue anyway? If she were a soldier, she would hate being at the facility. Helen waited for the lift to stop, the doors to open and the soldiers to step out of the elevator. "Thank you!" She followed them to Dr. Cheavers' office. Still angry, Helen waded into the good doctor. "What's the big idea leaving me to rot in my cell this morning? I missed breakfast."

"Mrs Fisher, please have a seat." Cheavers gestured the chair in front of her desk. Sitting down opposite Helen, Cheavers rested her elbows on the wooden surface. "I don't know how to tell you this if I'm honest. Now, don't be alarmed, but something happened to Kyle this morning." When Helen gasped, Cheavers put her hand up in reassurance. "Please, it's nothing horren-dous; he's perfectly fit and healthy...Probably a bit too healthy actually."

"What's that supposed to mean?" Helen's mind fired in a thousand different directions. Her hands covered her nose and mouth as she gasped. "Oh my God! He's dying, isn't he? It's okay, you can tell me...Just be honest with me, please."

Putting her hands out again, Cheavers tried shushing her. "Relax, Mrs Fisher, please. Kyle's not dying, I promise you. If anything, he's the opposite. His vitals are getting stronger by the day." She sighed, leaned back in her chair, and regarded Helen. "The thing is, Helen...The thing is, he's changing." The doctor leaned forward, her elbows back on the desk. "I know what you're going to say, you know that. Except last night, he changed, a lot, to the point where you might not recognise him anymore."

The corners of Helen's mouth rose. "Excuse me? Like how? He's a ten-year-old boy."

Getting to her feet, Cheavers invited Helen to join her in walking to Kyle's room. Out in the corridor, the doctor started explaining the situation. "Um, I think you need to prepare yourself." Cheavers reached the lift and called for it using her palm. "I really don't know how to say this, so I'll just come right out and say it."

The elevator doors opened and Cheavers stepped on first, turning to face Helen. She waited for Kyle's mum to get on before closing the doors. "He's aged overnight, okay? I know that when you left him last night he was a seemingly normal ten-year-old boy. This morning, he's a fit and healthy, and rather strapping fifteen year old lad. He's been fixated with his, you know what, his bits all morning. And I think he's developing bit of a crush on our Chloe."

Helen zoned out after the words 'fifteen year old lad'. Sure, Dr. Cheavers was talking, but Helen wasn't listening. Was Cheavers playing some sort of joke on her? Was she about to visit Kyle, only for Cheavers to shout, 'Surprise!?" Or was she being serious? And if true, how was it possible to leave her ten-year-old son overnight and return the following morning to find he'd aged five years overnight? Helen smiled, as the lift doors opened. "This is a joke, right? I must say, it's in bad taste. I'm worried enough about Kyle without you making jokes, Dr. Cheavers."

Cheavers stepped off the elevator and started walking. "Forgive me, Helen, but this isn't a joke. You know Kyle's infected by the spider bite, right?" Helen nodded, still smiling. "Well, this must be a side-effect of the infection, is my guess." The doctor took Helen along the familiar corridor until they came to Kyle's observation room door. "I'd prepare yourself if I were you. It's quite shocking."

The door hissed open, releasing the gases as Helen walked through, holding her breath. Before she turned and looked through the window into Kyle's room, she closed her eyes, praying it was a bad joke, that her little boy would be in there playing silly games by himself.

Sitting in the middle of the floor in front of a suited Chloe was a young man. Helen released her held breath. Tears welled up, as Helen let out a sob. Her little guy was a man, a fifteen-year-old young man, sitting there cross legged with cards in his hands, staring longingly across at the young and pretty Chloe. How had she missed five years of his life? She hadn't, of course, but nature had still taken those formative years away from him, and her, from them. Dr. Cheavers placed her hand on Helen's shoulder.

"I am sorry about this, Helen." Cheavers stood watching Kyle and Chloe with her. "Please know I'm doing all I can to understand this thing. We all are. Your son is our top priority."

Through the tears, which Helen wiped away, she asked, "How do you know he's fifteen?"

Glancing at Helen, Cheavers sighed. "The imaging scanner. There are markers we look for when ageing patients. At least he's fit and healthy, though, hmm?

There's always a silver lining, in every given situation. Kyle is strong and full of life. Look at him playing cards with Chloe. The two of them together, they're having so much fun."

Helen didn't care how much fun Kyle and Chloe were having. "Who looked after him when he found out he'd aged overnight?" Helen glared at Cheavers. "Who was here to calm him down, to stop him crying?"

"Chloe was here first thing." The doctor looked away as soon as she'd said Chloe's name.

"There's that name again!"

A female soldier entered carrying two suits, one for Helen and one for Cheavers. Helen quickly covered herself with the protective clothing, hood and visor. Without a word, she ordered the soldier to release the door. When she walked into Kyle's room, her son looked up from his cards and smiled. He didn't get up or rush over to her.

"Hey, mum!" His eyes went from her back to the cards in his hand.

"Hey mum?" Incensed, Helen strode over to Chloe, grabbed her by the shoulder and forced the young woman to her feet. "Thank you for your help this morning, Chloe, but your services are no longer required, okay?" She pushed Chloe in the back until she was through the doorway, into the observation room, when Helen hit the close button. By the time she'd closed the door, Kyle was on his feet. He was taller than her for the first time. "Look at you! Come here, give your mum a hug. I need it."

Kyle took her into a warm hug as asked. "It's okay, mum. I'm fine."

His voice was deep and strong, deeper than her husband's. "It's not okay, baby. You're not supposed to be a teenager yet." Helen broke the embrace and placed both palms on his cheeks. "You're still my little Kyle."

He smiled. "That's what Chloe says. I'll always be her little Kyle."

Pulling back, Helen let go of her son. "Is it now?" She turned and glared at Cheavers and Chloe through the window. "I mean it, Dr. Cheavers, I don't want Chloe anywhere near my son, do you understand? Anyone else but her. You know, you should've called me in straight away, not keep me cooped up in my cell. I should've been the one to comfort Kyle, not her."

Cheavers stepped back from the glass. "I don't think that's your choice to make, Helen." The doctor pointed behind her. "Look out!"

When Helen turned to Kyle, he was breathing deeply, turning red in the face. "Kyle, honey, what's the matter? You're hyperventilating, honey."

Kyle took two strides towards her. "You won't take

Chloe away from me, none of you will." He pushed Helen in the chest once, then again, pushing her in the direction of the door. "I want you and Chloe to get along, but if you can't do that, you can get out and leave us alone. I'm happy with Chloe, Mum, can't you see that? I'm stuck in this shithole against my wishes, but I'm making the most of it. And I'll be damned if you're going to ruin it for me."

The door behind Helen hissed and before she knew it, she was out in the observation room with Cheavers and Chloe. "Kyle!" The door closed on her. She dashed to the window. Kyle was pacing back and forth, flexing his fists while muttering to himself. "Kyle, honey, you don't mean that."

Without warning, Kyle went over to his bed, picked up the remote lying on his covers and launched it at the window. The glass didn't have time to crack and splinter; it smashed into millions of tiny fragments. "I want Chloe!"

With the window gone and Cheavers not wearing a protective suit, the doctor started panicking. "Oh my God! I'm exposed. I'm exposed. Damn it! Find me a suit, quick." Cheavers checked high and low for a hood and visor, anything she could use. "Security! There's been a breach. We're going to need to use all safety protocols."

She spoke into the radio. "I'm going into quarantine. I've been exposed."

Helen couldn't stand the anger in her son's eyes.

"Okay, Kyle. Chloe, you can stay." The strength he must hold was staggering. Most people, if they threw a remote at a window, the remote would bounce off it, or at the worst crack the glass. But Kyle had thrown it so hard, the glass had shattered, and the remote had hit the far wall and broken into pieces. The thought of being excluded from his life was too much to bear. If she had to share him with Chloe, then so be it.

"Dr. Cheavers, have you been bitten?" Aaron Pike's voice bounced around the room.

"No, but the window broke. I've been exposed to it. I'm breathing the same air." Cheavers rubbed her hair with one hand and held the radio in the other.

"You can relax on the quarantine. We've just had the results returned, this isn't a viral infection. Kyle's infected because he was bitten. Jenna was infected through sexual contact. There's no evidence that this is airborne. It's not a coronavirus. It's the only good news we have to share, so don't worry about quarantining yourself."

Relieved that Cheavers was safe, Helen took the man's information to mean that it was safe to take off her hood and visor. To be able to hug and kiss her son again was like all her birthdays and Christmases had come at once. Chloe followed her lead.

"Kyle!" Chloe stepped into Kyle's room through the broken window and ran into his arms. She was engulfed by him. "I won't ever leave you."

Incensed but trying to hide it, Helen waited for Kyle and Chloe to get acquainted in the flesh. They stopped short of kissing. It was obvious Chloe was into her son, her underage son. There was nothing Helen could do about it. "Hey you! Do you have one of those for me?"

"Sure thing. For you, always." Kyle pulled her in and engulfed her, too.

11

Aaron got up from his chair and stretched. He'd been hunkered down, writing his report all day. The only bit of excitement he'd had was informing Cheavers that she didn't need to isolate herself. Having the blood tests come back negative was a relief if nothing else. At least his team didn't need to worry about a disaster of pandemic proportions. No, all they had to do was worry about collecting all the spiders from Jackson's lab, and Zoe's two arachnoid babies. They should have been found, but Aaron tried not to worry. They would be located and destroyed eventually. "I'm done in. It's a shame they couldn't postpone the meeting until tomorrow morning. I might fall asleep in there."

Professor Charles 'Charlie' Roache finished packing his case, prepped for the meeting with Colonel Trantor and his superiors, up to and including defence secretary, Ben Willard. "You and me both. At least we've got some good news to give them. It might lighten the mood for a change; they're such a stuffy bunch."

He had to give it to Roache, Aaron had thought the geneticist would be stuffy and serious. Not a bit of it. Roache didn't take himself too seriously, constantly sending himself up. "Yeah, well, I guess they're under a lot of pressure. I wouldn't want to be the one to have to tell the prime minister and public that we might have an epidemic of half-human / half spider babies taking over the country, would you?"

Roache smiled. "Any other time and that sentence would be straight out of some nasty horror B-Movie." He shook his head. "Who'd have thought it would come to this. I tell you, it's a crazy world we live in. And if giant man-spiders are the thing of tomorrow, I don't want a part of it. Spiders freak me out, but this...being sucked dry from the inside out, well, it doesn't even beg to think about, does it?" The geneticist glanced at Aaron and winced. "Oh shit, I'm so sorry. I completely forgot you were sucked on. Forgive me?"

Like Aaron needed reminding of being attacked by two of Hardcastle's offspring. The wound on his leg was all but gone. The one on his chest still hurt to the touch, even twelve days later. "Hey, I'm with you. I wish I hadn't agreed to try and find Jackson. If I hadn't, I wouldn't be down here in this fucking prison. All I want to do is hug my wife."

The door to the office opened prior to Colonel Trantor entering, flanked by two soldiers, who stood behind him, their legs apart, arms behind their backs. "Gentlemen, it's time for our weekly update. Bring everything you need. We're meeting with everyone, from the defence Secretary, Ben Willard down. And Mr. Pike, be on your best behaviour, or I'll see to it that you spend the rest of your stay here locked in your room, do I make myself clear?"

Picking up his case, Aaron nodded. "Sure thing, boss." His tone was sarcastic. Who the hell was the colonel to tell him how to behave? The colonel's seniors were less than cooperative during the last meeting, when Aaron had told them how imperative it was that they catch the spiders. They didn't seem to understand that if even one of those arachnids were left, it could cause a public health crisis the likes of which they had never seen before. The rate at which they could reproduce meant they were in a race against the clock.

After following the colonel to the lift, up to level four, Aaron put his case on the edge of a conference table long enough for twelve people. He took to his usual seat next to Trantor, who was sitting at the head of the table, opposite the TV screen and camera. Aaron leaned back in his seat and waited for the TV to fill up with the meeting's hosts.

Three faces appeared on the screen. The first Aaron recognised as the young and charismatic Ben Willard, the Secretary of State for Defence, who had appeared on the news a lot in recent years as part of his role as Home Secretary, then Defence Secretary. He was going in the wrong direction under Prime Minister Hugh Dawson. The second face Aaron recognised from the previous meetings: General Iain Hague, the most patronising and obnoxious man Aaron had ever met.

"Major General Urban, I'm so pleased you could make it," Trantor started, sucking up to the third face on the screen, his immediate senior. "I was told you were busy. And Mr. Defence Secretary, it's an honour to finally meet you. I have with me my top two researchers, Geneticist Charles Roache and Entomologist, Aaron Pike. They've both been working tirelessly to find a solution to our situation."

General Hague tutted with his arms crossed in one corner of the TV. "Just get on with the presentation, Trantor. We haven't got all day, unlike you down there in that pit."

It was the first time Aaron had seen Trantor nervous. He liked it, hoping there would be more outbursts from

Hague later. "May I, colonel?" When Trantor took his seat, Aaron got up and faced the three men on TV. He cleared his throat. "Good evening, gentlemen. I'm Aaron Pike, an entomologist over at the Royal Entomological Society in St Albans. Approximately two weeks ago I was tasked with locating missing arachnologist, Professor Philip Jackson. After his less than graceful departure from the BAS, Jackson took his team and set up his own society. Because no one at the RES was really working with him, we didn't know that he'd shut up shop and had started a new project in the basement of a derelict factory in central London. We found out that he'd started a partnership with disgraced geneticist Jonas Eckstein. In the basement they had over two-hundred-and-fifty non indigenous exotic spiders."

The general cut in. "Excuse me, Mr. Pike, but when are you going to get to the point?"

"Forgive me, general, but Mr. Pike is giving you the background to this situation." The colonel nodded at Aaron to continue, almost apologising for the interruption.

"Right, I'll get to the point, shall I?" He checked the general's response. "The point is this: Eckstein and Jackson have genetically altered an undisclosed number of these spiders, the bites of which infect a human host and turn them into what we now call Arachnoids, half human, half spider hybrids. The main problem we have is that we don't know how many spiders they've experimented on, and we don't know where they are, or how long they've been missing for. Jackson and an urban photographer, Zoe Hardcastle were both bitten by black widows, and we all know what happened to them. Right now, there could be any number of transformations occurring in the London area."

It was the defence secretary's turn to chip in. "Surely not. We would know about any of these so-called transformations, wouldn't we? Anyone with an ounce of intelligence would consult their GP, or go to A and E, wouldn't they?"

"I wouldn't count on that, Mr, Willard." Aaron paused for effect and to catch his breath. "Both Jackson and Zoe Hardcastle reported an overwhelming desire to reproduce. Jackson impregnated a young woman, while Hardcastle went to great lengths to get herself pregnant, going as far as eating the father to keep him quiet. I believe this overwhelming need to reproduce would stop the infected from seeking help."

With a snort of derision, General Hague tutted. "Right, and you know this, how? I only deal in facts, Mr. Pike, not conjecture or beliefs. You can't possibly know that. The defence secretary is right, anyone bitten by a spider, who starts to see their body changing would seek medical assistance. I've had our people monitoring radio chatter for the past ten days and nothing. This tells me there aren't 'any number of transformations happening right now'. So, do you have any real evidence for us today?"

The general's attitude was making Aaron's palm twitch. "You mean apart from Jackson and Hardcastle's hideously deformed corpses downstairs? You've seen the video footage of Jackson changing, general. How about the little lad we have locked up here who has more than likely been bitten by a Huntsman spider? His arm is almost entirely infected, and he has aged five years overnight. Do you want to hear my theory on that?"

"Not if it's just a theory, no. We need solid proof, Mr. Pike."

"How about Jenna Martin, the unfortunate economics student who slept with Jackson? Four months later she gave birth to an egg sac. For the best part of four months she was comatose, until the egg hatched. How about this for proof, General Hague? You know what, I didn't ask to be involved in this. I would much rather be tucked up in bed with Lily, who, I hasten to add, I haven't spoken since being abducted and brought here."

There was a long silence. Aaron tried his best to calm his temper by taking deep breaths. The thought of holding Lily hurt. The senior faces on the TV said nothing. They were probably waiting for him to continue. To show them he'd finished his section of the meeting, Aaron sat back down next to Colonel Trantor.

The defence secretary was the first to break the silence, clearing his throat. "Mr. Pike, I'm interested to hear more about this Jenna Martin, is it? Please, tell us how this infection has affected her."

12

Jenna couldn't get comfortable. Lying on her side to stop the pain, she sat up and dangled her legs over the edge of her bed. The cysts on her back were getting larger and more painful by the day. What had started out as one cyst was now eight and seemed to be growing. Jenna had asked Dr. Cheavers why they couldn't drain them. The doctor's response had not filled her with much confidence; she'd told Jenna that it wouldn't help, that the cysts would only fill back up, and might be more painful the second time round. Cheavers had reassured Jenna that she was her top priority, that she was doing all she could to solve the puzzle of infection.

"Jenna, are you alright?" Dr. Cheavers was outside in the observation room wearing only pyjamas, much like Jenna was. Gone was the protective suit. "Do you need more painkillers? I can get you some paracetamol if you need them, or something stronger."

With care, Jenna got to her feet and walked slowly over to the window. "No, taking all these painkillers is wreaking havoc on my bowels. When are these things going to pop, or whatever? They're getting bigger and fatter each day. I just want to go home, back to my family, don't you get that?"

The doctor stepped to the side of the window, opened the door and entered, the first time without wearing her hood and visor. Cheavers went to Jenna's side, guided her back to the bed and made her lie on her side again. "I get it, Jenna. I really do. I don't want to be here either. I'm trapped as much as you are. Everyone here is."

Being upright was more painful for Jenna than lying down. She let Dr. Cheavers take her back to bed, the pressure in her cysts too much to bear. She stared up at her doctor. "What do you mean everyone is? This is a military compound, isn't it?"

"Sure, but all the soldiers you see here are every bit as much victims as you or I. The only person who has access all areas is Colonel Trantor and Professor Roache. The highest any of us can go is floor two. So you see we're all trapped, just like you." She stroked Jenna's hair.

Jenna wondered what Cheavers' story was. "Why are you here?"

With a sigh, Cheavers stopped stroking her hair and stared longingly at the far side of the room. "I was seconded against my will, Jenna, like everyone else. When you gave birth to that...Thing, I put a call out over the radio that we had a situation, that we needed to quarantine the area. I did what I was supposed to. I made sure we sealed off the area. A few hours into self-isolation inside the room with you these guys in white suits arrived. We were all rounded up, put in helicopters on the hospital roof, and flown over here."

"And where is here?" Jenna was starting to feel sorry for the doctor. If Jenna had not presented herself at the A and E ward, Cheavers wouldn't be a prisoner with her.

"We were blindfolded, so I don't know exactly." Cheavers turned and looked down at Jenna with a sympathetic smile. "Anyway, we were put in isolation here for four weeks until I gave the all-clear, at which point I took on the role as your physician. I've learned so much from you, Jenna. We wouldn't have half as much knowledge about this infection without you." Cheavers stroked her hair again. "I know it's hard, but please try and get some rest. Here, let me make it more comfortable for you."

Jenna lay on her side, enjoying the fuss being made

of her. Cheavers put Jenna's pillows behind her back, so she could relax a bit more without squashing the cysts. "When are my family getting here, doctor?" She longed to see her parents again. Jenna had begged Dr. Cheavers to ask the colonel to allow her parents down to visit her.

Cheavers sat up and rubbed her face, then let out a long sigh. She got up and stared down at Jenna, her eyes sad. "I'm sorry! I didn't want to tell you this, but you deserve to know. They're not coming, Jenna. Colonel Trantor told them they would have to stay down here with you until you recovered. I'm afraid they weren't prepared to. They send their love, though, honey. Why don't you focus on getting some sleep, yeah? You're going to need the rest before you get better. I'll ask the colonel to keep trying, okay?"

She couldn't believe it. Surely her mum or dad would gladly stay with her? Wouldn't they? How could they let her stay here by herself? Jenna fought back the tears, not wanting the doctor to witness her vulnerability. When the doctor squeezed her shoulder before disappearing in the next room, she let out a sob. How could her parents leave her like this? Jenna didn't expect both of them to stay with her, but either her mum or dad could have. It wasn't fair! Jenna was supposed to be enjoying university life, or she should say her summer holidays. No, Jenna had to escape, somehow.

13

"Wait! So you're saying this poor girl not only gave birth to an egg sac, but now she's carrying eight unfertilised egg sacs on her back?" The defence secretary pulled a disgusted face. "Why? What are these new sacs for? And how do you know they're not just cysts?"

Aaron put his hand out to silence Roache, who was about to say something. "We know they're egg sacs because Dr. Cheavers analysed them. They're full of amniotic fluid, sir. Why they're forming on Jenna Martin's back we can only speculate about. The sacs are a lot smaller than the one she birthed. We would expect the babies to be a lot smaller. The baby that came out of the bigger sac was about the size of a grapefruit. We would expect these to be more in line with normal spiders."

The general interrupted. "Again, Mr. Pike, this is all conjecture and ifs and maybes. We really need to know what happens if this Jenna Martin gets impregnated by an infected host, don't we? Then we would have our evidence."

Silence. Aaron went from the general, to the defence secretary to Roache, and finally the colonel. They were all busy thinking. "Um, what do you mean by that, general?"

"You have an infected teenager down there, right?"

Aaron didn't like where the conversation was going. "Yeah, so?"

"Jesus! Do I need to spell it out for you?" The general wasn't asking a rhetorical question. "Get these two together, see what happens. If she's carrying eggs on her back, fill them up and see what comes out. Am I being clear enough for you?"

He couldn't believe the words coming out of the general's mouth. "Um no! That's unbelievably unethical, general. You're suggesting impregnating Jenna intentionally for research purposes." The words were disgusting, just saying them out loud. "No way! That's not happening. I'm here to try and help Jenna and Kyle, that's my remit."

The defence secretary smiled. "Your remit? Mr Pike, your remit is what we say it is, do you understand? If we want you to put these two together, that is what will happen. The research facility you're in is financed by the British government. If I give you the order, I expect you to carry it out, or I'll have the colonel keep you in isolation down there. We're in charge of this situation, got it?"

What an arsehole! Aaron nodded. "Understood sir." He sat back in his chair with his arms crossed, listening to the conversations between those on the television and Trantor and Roache. He was furious. Luckily, the colonel steered the conversation away from getting Jenna pregnant, and onto something completely different.

The geneticist, Roache took over, detailing the autopsy of Jackson and Hardcastle. Roache explained how Jackson and Hardcastle's bodies had transformed, about how their bodies were split into a cephalothorax and abdomen, and how the six new legs had erupted through the ribcage, killing Jackson. "Hardcastle, on the other hand survived the transformation process." Roache went on to explain the similarities between humans and spiders, their anatomy, and the differences. The main difference, Roache stipulated, was where the Arachnoids spun their webs from.

"Hang on, I thought spiders spin their webs from

their backsides?" The defence secretary seemed puzzled. "Am I missing something here?"

"No sir, the glands were found in Jackson and Hardcastle's throats. They spin their webs from their mouths, making these things efficient killing machines. Combining human and arachnid DNA is, frankly, genius. This is why it's imperative we locate these missing spiders, and Hardcastle's two offspring. May I ask how the search is going?"

The general prattled on about how he had four teams scouring every inch of the abandoned tunnels beneath the streets of London. For ten days they'd been down there and nothing. "Of course it could take weeks, maybe months to cover the whole area, but we'll find those two freaks, don't you worry about that."

Colonel Trantor put his hand up. "Sir, might it be a good idea to enlist the help of civilians in the search for the missing spiders?" He put his hand down after a glare from General Hague. "It was just a thought, sir. I was only thinking aloud."

"Mr. Pike, Mr. Roache, you may both leave us now." The general's tone was forceful.

Not needing to be asked twice, Aaron picked up his file and followed Roache out into the corridor. Instead of going with the geneticist, Aaron stayed behind, trying to listen into the conversation inside. "Just go, I'll be right behind you," he told Roache, who tried to get him to leave before they both wound up in trouble. Once Roache had left, Aaron pressed his ear to the door. There was a raised voice, but Aaron couldn't make out specifics. It sounded like Trantor was getting grilled by Hague and Willard.

The door opened while Aaron had his ear to it. Aaron attempted to make out he wasn't eavesdropping. He failed. "Hey, I'm worried for Jenna, okay? After what Hague said-"

Trantor closed the door and started walking with Aaron. "Seriously? Do you really think I'm going to authorise that? You disappoint me, Mr. Pike. I thought you had more respect for me than that. Hague can come down here and do it himself. I'm not getting involved. Go on back to your office, would you? You have important work to be getting on with. And don't worry, nothing's going to happen to Jenna, I promise."

Relieved, Aaron got on the lift with the colonel. He was grateful that Trantor had principles, even if his bosses didn't. Hague and Willard were safe where they were, they had not met the pretty young student, or the cute kid, Kyle. They were both just names to the likes of Hague and Willard. Aaron stepped off the elevator two floors below the colonel.

14

Melissa Poulsen rolled onto her back, her breathing heavy. It was hard work fucking in a two berth tent, but it sure was fun trying. She hadn't had that much fun with her boyfriend, Oren in months, years even. Maybe it was being out in the middle of nowhere, in a big old wood that did it, made her horny. Earlier in the evening, Oren had taken her clothes off in the middle of the woods, under the cover of the trees. With the gentle orange glow of the fire, she'd succumbed to Oren's charms. Why had they not gone camping together before?

"Damn, Mel, that was amazing." Oren, lying next to her on his back, chuckled to himself. "We really ought to do this more often, babe, you know?"

She couldn't agree more. "Uh-huh! Being here in the

woods makes me hotter than-" She paused, staring up at the fabric roof of the tent. The sound of a baby crying made Melissa sit up. "Do you hear that?" She shushed Oren when he started talking. Nothing. Melissa lay back down next to her boyfriend.

The baby crying was louder. "There! Did you hear it?" Melissa sat up and started pulling her knickers up her legs when the crying grew in volume. She stopped getting dressed, stopped everything, listening for the baby crying. "What is that, Oren?" She whispered so quietly as to barely hear it herself.

When the crying sound came a fourth time it was mixed with a kind of hissing sound. Whatever it was, it creeped Melissa out enough for her to reach across for her T shirt and put it on. Oren followed her lead, putting on a pair of shorts and a T shirt as quietly as he could. Instead of talking, Melissa and Oren stayed perfectly silent, listening.

The ceiling of the tent moved, liked something was touching it. The something was sharp, tearing the canvas. Melissa screamed at the black sharp instrument, quickly lying on her back, praying it didn't continue its descent. Oren lay next to her, trying to dodge it, while holding her.

Pulling out, the sharp instrument disappeared for a second, before something landed on top of the tent, dropping in between Melissa and Oren. Melissa tried to find a way outside, but with the huge object on top of the ten it was stifling and cramped. Whatever it was kept moving. Melissa couldn't see a thing, until an orange glow saved her. The fire was still burning. She crawled in the direction of the fire, found the door, and unzipped it.

On her elbows and knees, Melissa crawled along the dry mud until she felt the warmth of the fire. Behind her, the thing attacking them was screaming and thrashing about. When Melissa turned, Oren was crawling out of the tent when he cried out in pain. "Oren!"

Something had speared Oren's leg. Melissa still couldn't identify their attacker. It was fighting with the tent while torturing Oren. Her boyfriend waved at her, telling her to stay back. He was grimacing at the pain, their attacker twisting his leg in every direction.

Getting to her feet, the fire behind her, Melissa finally identified their attacker. Her mouth hung open as eight legs appeared from the tent. Or rather six legs and two arms with hands and fingers. It was hideous, shiny and black, with fangs and a strangely human face. Melissa screamed higher and longer than she'd ever screamed in her life.

The spider thing yanked its claw out of Oren's leg

and stabbed him in the back, blood gushing out of her boyfriend's mouth. "No! Oren!" Melissa wanted to run to him, to help him, but her legs wouldn't carry her there. They remained steadfast.

Melissa watched as the spider thing hovered its fangs above Oren's head. When it attacked, it did so with such speed that Melissa almost missed it, until it was sucking on her boyfriend's brains, its fangs deep inside his skull. From where she was standing, Melissa could see the expression of pain and disbelief in Oren's eyes until they rolled back in his head. Wrinkles formed the more the spider thing sucked on him. "Oren, please!"

"G-go!" Was the last word Oren would say.

Melissa turned and fled. Spider Thing took no time in chasing her, its claws thudding on the earth behind her. Each thud gained in both volume and bass, meaning it was gaining on her. In the woods alone without a light source, Melissa stood no chance. Something latched onto her back, yanked and forced her to the ground. Spider Thing crawled over her, crying and hissing at the same time. Melissa wanted to close her ears.

Confused, Melissa felt sick when Spider Thing started wrapping her in webbing, spinning her round horizontally until she was covered head to toe in sticky webs. She tried screaming but the webbing covering her mouth and nose muffled it. Only her eyes and forehead remained unwrapped. It wasn't long before the monster dragged her along the mud.

After what felt like five minutes, Spider Thing stopped dragging her. Melissa scanned the area, her eyes darting from left to right, up and down. They were in some kind of outhouse, a barn of some sort. It was definitely a building made of wood.

Spider Thing cried and hissed louder than before. Melissa heard movement in the background. Behind some hay bales, a shadow moved. The shadow was big, bigger than Spider Thing. She gasped when another spider thing emerged, only bigger and more superior. It was twice the size of her spider thing. It had to be six feet tall.

When the two spider things greeted one another, her spider thing tugged on the webbing and dragged Melissa over to them. She was being offered as a gift. Melissa tried screaming, for the good it would do, but couldn't. She was too terrified to scream even.

Too scared to wrestle with the webbing, Melissa's eyes grew large when the bigger spider thing approached her, its fat legs thudding on the ground until it loomed over her. Its fangs were twice the length of her spider thing's, hovering above her.

It was over so fast. Its fangs pierced her skull and

sank deep into Melissa's brain. Why wasn't she dead? Melissa wished she was, feeling it drinking her very soul. Every gulp the spider thing took made Melissa more drowsy. How had it come to this? Why was she not warned that there were monsters. Real monsters. If she'd known, Melissa would have stayed indoors with Oren. Melissa's peripheral vision blurred and went dark, leaving her last image the spider thing's bright red chest. There was a red hour glass shape on its chest.

15

Aaron rubbed his eyes before stretching. Since leaving the conference room earlier, he had not left his office. Colonel Trantor had asked him to write his report sooner than expected. Originally not due until a week Monday, Trantor had pulled it forward. It was due in two days and Aaron had only begun writing it. Depriving himself of sleep wouldn't help his report. Checking the clock on his monitor, it was approaching midnight.

The radio sitting on his desk crackled. "Aaron, are you still in your office?"

He picked up the handheld radio. "That's affirmative, Eleanor. I thought you'd be in bed by now. What's up?" He placed the device back on the desk.

"I was on my way back to my room when I stopped

to see how Jenna's doing." Cheavers paused for a couple of seconds. "Can you come and take a look at something for me?"

Switching his PC off, Aaron agreed to meet Cheavers in Jenna's observation room in five minutes. He wondered what it could be. Hadn't the poor girl been through enough already? The worst Jenna had done was sleep with a guy. It took him three and a half minutes to walk the corridors and take the lift before using his palm to open the door.

Doctor Cheavers was standing in front of the window. "Hey!" She glanced over at him, beckoning him to join her. "Come! Listen to this."

Standing next to the doctor, Aaron obliged, listening. Coming from inside Jenna's room was a kind of scratching sound, mixed with a kind of purr. Aaron shuddered. "What is that?"

Taking her leave, Cheavers walked to the control panel next to the door to Jenna's room. "Jenna's making that sound." She opened the door and walked through, requesting Aaron join her. "You don't have to pussy foot around, Aaron. She's fast asleep. Right now, she's in a REM phase. Nothing will wake her up."

Aaron still tiptoed over to Jenna's bed, where the poor girl was lying on her side facing him. Squatting in front of Jenna, he listened to the sound again, the scratchy purr. Louder, it creeped him out even more. Jenna was making it using the back of her throat. "That's the weirdest fucking snore I've ever heard."

Squatting next to Aaron, Cheavers leaned in closer to Jenna's mouth. "I don't think it is a snore. Could it be a call of some kind? I've been reading about how spiders use mating cries to attract the males. I don't know, am I reading too much into it?"

He'd heard the sound of a wolf spider purring before. Jenna's noise was similar in many ways, only more scratchy. A lot of insects and arachnids had mating calls, sounds they often made using their legs or other body parts. It was not too hard to believe that Jenna was making one of these mating calls. The girl was changing daily, into what, he couldn't guess. "It's possible. But if it is a mating cry, you know what that means, don't you?" He waited for Cheavers to nod. "There are more of them out there. I mean, as far as we know for sure, there are Hardcastle's two babies, right? Well, unless there are more bite victims, Jenna can only be calling the male baby." An image of one of the babies biting his leg flashed in his mind. "But that's only if Jenna is calling for it. And it's a big if."

"I guess we'll never know." Cheavers stood and went to pull the sheet over Jenna when she stopped, pulling it back instead. "Oh no! There are more sacs."

The smell was bad enough, without the image of twelve egg sacs on Jenna's back. They were all oval in shape, milky white and bulbous. Aaron wanted to throw up just smelling and staring at them. "She only had eight earlier. That's four more in a few hours." He would do anything to take the pain away from Jenna. It was a shame she was such a valuable asset to his research.

Still squatting, Aaron jumped when Jenna's eyes opened suddenly. She lay there staring through him. "Jenna? It's Aaron." He fell on his backside when Jenna sat upright in her bed. Aaron had to move when she flung her legs over the edge before standing. Shimmying back to the main door, Aaron had to warn Cheavers to move when Jenna started after her.

He didn't know how, but Aaron found himself out in the observation room with Cheavers on his bum. He accepted Cheavers' help getting up and joined the doctor in watching Jenna through the glass. "What the hell was that?" Jenna was staring at him while making the purring sound with her throat. It was not a noise Aaron could emulate.

16

Laurence 'Larry' Prescott awoke to the sound of a baby crying in the distance. His old bones creaking and his bladder calling to be emptied, he hoisted himself out of bed and went to the bathroom to take a leak before he wet himself. When he went back to his bedroom, he could still hear the crying outside. Ordinarily, it wouldn't bother him, except Larry lived a ways from his nearest neighbour in an old farm that had been passed down from one generation to the next. Why was there a crying baby out there?

Grumbling to himself, Larry put on some slacks over his underwear and a T shirt and sweater over his vest. Finally, he sat on his bed and put on an old pair of wellies he kept by the side of his bed in case of emergency exits. Being seventy-five and forgetful meant he might need to make a hasty exit one day. "Let's see what you're doing out there, shall we?"

In the kitchen, Larry put on the light and hunted for the front door key. Why didn't he keep it in a safe place? Walking slowly, he let himself out into the chilly night air. Even with a sweater on, he shivered. The baby crying was louder than inside, creepier. Listening while heading in its direction, Larry noticed a hissing sound mixed in with the crying.

His huge barn was up ahead. The crying was getting louder still. Larry kept moving forward, heading for the barn. It had to be in there, the door was open, after he'd shut it earlier. Larry stopped a few feet away from the outhouse. "Whoever you are, you've come to the wrong place. I'm armed out here. Why don't you come on out, hmm?"

Nothing. The crying stopped as soon as he spoke. There was something moving inside the barn. "Don't go doing anything stupid, do you hear me? The police are on their way." If someone was in his barn, why were they staying quiet? "If you need somewhere to sleep tonight, all you have to do is ask."

If his wife, Daisy were alive, she would be begging him to phone the police, to leave it to them. She always was nervous; she hated living so far out in the middle of the sticks. Still, London was only an hour's drive away, which was plenty close enough for Larry. Thinking how stupid he was being, Larry swallowed before making his way inside the barn.

Without his torch, with only the moon lighting his way, Larry was pretty much blind in the barn. Not that it mattered; he knew every inch of the outhouse he'd helped his grandfather build all those moons ago. Edging his way to the centre, Larry jumped at a noise. "Who's in here? Show yourself, damn it! This isn't funny."

The screech sent Larry staggering backwards until he lost his footing. He fell onto his backside with a thud. Something was advancing on him, but he couldn't see what it was. Shimmying away, Larry hit the barn wall. He turned his head slowly at the figure sitting beside him. He wanted to scream, yet no sound came out.

Whoever it was, she was covered in what he could only describe as webbing. Her face was shrivelled up, wrinkly, but different. The woman cocooned in the webbing wasn't an old lady, far from it. Up closer, the woman seemed almost drained of life, like something had sucked it out of her.

His focus went from the dead woman in his barn to whatever was stalking him. It appeared in the shadows, big with eight, no, six legs and two arms. Larry wanted to be anywhere but his barn. "There's a good boy. You won't hurt me, would you?" It continued its slow advance, its legs thudding on the ground.

Another noise confused Larry. The monster in front of him stopped its advance and turned to face...An even bigger monster. Larry gulped at the sheer size of it. They were of the same species, it seemed. Fear propelled him to try and escape. Larry got as far as standing when webbing shot out of the first monster's mouth, covering him in the stickly substance. It secured him to the wood of the wall, the webbing covering his entire body, leaving only his head free. Larry tried fighting it, but the webbing constricted with every movement.

All Larry could do was watch the two monsters. The smaller one approached the bigger one. They were all legs, literally. When the smaller monster straddled the bigger one, Larry understood what he'd done. He'd interrupted their mating ritual. But the way the smaller monster was going about it...It was almost...Larry shook his head. It was almost human, the monster using its front arms to grip the waist of the bigger monster.

Out of nowhere, the smaller monster paused, turned and started sniffing the air. It angered the larger monster. The smaller one fled the barn, leaving Larry with only the angry one. He held his breath when it screeched and made its way toward him.

17

Kyle opened his eyes when the lights overhead flickered to life. It couldn't be morning already, he couldn't have been asleep more than a couple of hours. Tired and drowsy still, he pulled the bed sheet back and his breath caught at the sight of his arms. They were both grey with flecks of black, his skin a strange texture, not flesh. Wanting to call out for Chloe, Kyle stopped himself. He was a big boy now. Big boys didn't cry out for their mummies or anyone. "No! Be adult about this, Kyle Fisher. You're a grown up now."

Only yesterday, after his daily trip to the scanning machine, Dr. Cheavers had informed him that he was officially an adult, with the fit and healthy body of an eighteen year old. His mum had cried at the sight of him when she'd come to visit. Kyle hated seeing his mum cry; it made him feel bad, because he was the cause, or rather the stupid spider bite was.

Getting up, wearing his pyjamas Kyle strolled over to his bathroom, where he yawned and took a leak at the same time. It couldn't be time to get up. His body told him otherwise. After relieving himself, Kyle took his time putting his penis away, staring at it and grinning. Oh, what he wanted to do with it to Chloe. The only problem he had was privacy. If he could only get some alone time with her, Kyle knew Chloe felt the same way. Or at least he hoped she did. On his way over to the basin, Kyle noticed some strange hairs on his legs.

Bending over, he rubbed the hairs, noting how coarse they were, thicker than his normal leg hairs. One of them pricked him, cutting into his thumb. "Ow! You bastard!" He sucked the blood from his digit. "I wonder what you're all about?" He'd found himself talking to inanimate objects often.

The grey was taking over. In the mirror above the basin, Kyle unbuttoned his pyjama top and studied his chest. The grey covered both shoulders and had spread over his taut pectorals, stretching over half of his abdominals. His legs were still his own pasty white. The doctor had warned him that his entire body would turn grey eventually. He'd asked her what would happen then? She'd assured him that she was doing everything she could to find a cure. When she'd left without answering his question, he'd left it. He kind of knew the answer. The way his mum kept bursting into tears on him, it wasn't good news.

Kyle played with his mouth, opening it and closing. It felt strange, like there was something behind his teeth. As hard as he tried, Kyle couldn't shake the strange sensation. Or maybe there was padding behind his teeth or something? There was no one he could talk to about it; no one had been through what he was going through.

A hissing sound next door made Kyle wander through to his room, expecting to find Chloe waiting for him. When the room was empty, he frowned. "Hello? Chloe?" The door was open, the sterilising agent hissing. Strange! The door was never left open or unattended, ever. He crept up to the doorframe and poked his head through the gas. No one was there.

Curious, Kyle stepped into the corridor alone for the first time since being brought to the 'hospital'. With caution, he wandered out of the door that opened when he reached it. What was going on? Who was controlling the doors? Going through, Kyle kept walking until he reached the elevator. After the door opened for him, he stepped on board.

The lift stopped and the doors opened. Kyle stepped

off and followed the automatically opening doors until he arrived at one that remained closed. He used his palm to open it, but nothing happened. The panel turned neither green nor red. "Hello?"

What was going on? The door hissed and slid across. After he'd traversed the sterilising gas, Kyle found himself in an observation room identical to the one outside his room. Colonel Trantor was standing in front of the window. "Colonel Trantor? Where am I?"

Colonel Trantor turned to face him. "Good morning, Kyle. How are you feeling today?" He turned back to the window not interested in his reply. "I've got someone I want you to meet." He gestured the person in the room on the opposite side of the glass. "This is Jenna."

Kyle had never seen a girl as beautiful as her before. With long blonde hair and an oh so pretty face, Jenna surpassed even Chloe. Kyle licked his lips, which were so dry. "I've seen her before." And he had. But where? Kyle had to adjust his crotch. "She's beautiful."

"She is, isn't she? Jenna's waiting for you, Kyle." Colonel Trantor put his hand on Kyle's shoulder. "You're officially an adult now, Kyle. Dr. Cheavers shared the wonderful news with me this morning."

Unable to take his eyes away from the eggs on Jenna's back, Kyle had to meet Jenna. "She's ripe, colonel." He didn't even know where the words were coming from; he only knew he had to get in there and be with Jenna. She was so beautiful lying on top of the sheets, her lumpy white back enticing him to meet her. "Can I go in?"

With a knowing smile, Colonel Trantor turned to face him. "You won't be needing those pyjamas, Kyle. Why don't you take them off? I'll hold on to them for you until you're done meeting with her." He stepped up to Kyle, helping him take off his clothing.

After handing the colonel his pyjama top, Kyle pulled his trousers down and gave them to his host. Standing naked next to the colonel, he waited until the door was open. He took a deep breath and went through the sterilising gas. Inside, Jenna was still lying on her bed, her eyes closed. "Jenna?" He started walking over to her.

When he was half way across the room, Jenna's eyes opened. She balked, sitting up and shimmying back against the wall. "I'm not yours." She shook her head. "You'll not have me. He won't like that. I'm his."

"Whose Jenna? Whose are you?" The colonel was inside the room, but stayed back, out of the reach of the CCTV camera.

"I don't know who he is, only that I meet him in my dreams." Jenna clung to the wall.

Kyle didn't like the idea of someone else having

D.C. BROCKWELL

Jenna. "You're the most beautiful woman I've ever seen, Jenna. Please, can I sit on the bed with you?" Jenna shook her head in defiance. It looked like Kyle wouldn't get to be with her. Anger built up in his gut. If he couldn't have Chloe, he sure as hell would have Jenna. "You're perfect! In every way. Please, Jenna, let's get comfortable." He made his way to the bed, sitting on the edge.

When he patted the sheet, Jenna seemed to relax, gradually sitting next to him. Kyle put his hand out and touched one of the eggs on her back. The sac was soft to the touch, although it hurt Jenna. He touched her cheek with his palm. She shied away from it, telling him that she wasn't his to take. Behind a smile, Kyle was seething.

With the speed and agility even he didn't realise he had, Kyle pinned Jenna to the wall, making sure she lay on her side. Kyle didn't want to hurt the egg sacs. Jenna struggled. She kept saying she wasn't his, that he wouldn't like it. Not that Kyle cared; he had only one thing on his mind: Jenna was going to be his.

18

"Okay, let's try and figure this thing out, shall we?" Aaron was pacing over his own footsteps in the conference room with Dr. Cheavers and Professor Roache. They were both sitting at the table, their heads in their hands, having been discussing the virus since six o'clock. Aaron noted it was half past nine. "So, Jackson gets bitten by a black widow and starts transforming into an Arachnoid, right? While his physiology is changing, he goes to a bar and picks up Jenna Martin. They have sex and four months later, she gives birth to an egg sac."

"Correct, so far." Professor Roache looked up at Aaron. "An infected man impregnates a human woman, transforming her physiology, too."

"But what I don't get is the eggs on Jenna's back."

Cheavers threw her hands up. "Why didn't Hardcastle have egg sacs growing on her? I just can't get my head round this."

Aaron nodded. "I know. It's throwing me, too." He walked back and forth a couple of times while thinking. "Zoe Hardcastle was bitten by one of Jackson's mutated spiders, yes?" They agreed. "She was in hospital for a few days in a coma. Then she comes out and returns home. A few days after that she goes to a nightclub and picks up Steven Hack. They have sex, and an uninfected Steven impregnates Hardcastle." He was thinking it through, still pacing. "When we were down in the subway, there were eight sacs in total. So, why did Jenna Martin only give birth to one? Why did Hardcastle give birth to eight?"

Cheavers lifted her head, her eyes wide and hopeful. "Hardcastle was infected, and Jenna wasn't." She got up from her seat and started pacing with Aaron. "Hear me out: okay, so, Hardcastle lays eight eggs, yes? And Jenna only has one. Maybe, because Hardcastle was infected before she was impregnated, her physiology had already changed enough to maximise her egg production? Jenna was human when she met Jackson. Maybe her physiology is still so human it can only support production of one, or maybe two egg sacs?"

Hitting the table with his fist, Roache ended

Cheavers' thinking out loud. "That's it! It has to be. Hardcastle was infected, Jenna wasn't. A human body couldn't produce that many eggs. Aaron, I think we've cracked it. When you write your report, be sure to-"

"But it still doesn't explain the eggs on Jenna's back." Aaron wanted to think they'd cracked it, but too many questions remained unanswered. "None of this explains these bloody sacs on her back. Why didn't Hardcastle have eggs on her back?"

The jubilance was short-lived.

"These spiders were genetically mutated, right?" Cheavers' mind was firing in a thousand different directions at once. "So, as far as we know a person has to be bitten by one of these modified spiders to be infected. I mean, Aaron was bitten by one of Hardcastle's offspring and nothing. Being bitten by an Arachnoid doesn't infect people, only being bitten by one of these experimental subjects. And the eggs on Jenna's back are very different from the one she birthed, yes? If the eggs on her back were to be fertilised, the offspring would be a hell of a lot smaller than the one that came out of Jenna's main egg."

Aaron was starting to understand the direction Cheavers was going in. "It's evolution. Survival of the species. If Arachnoids can't make more of their own kind by biting hosts-"

"Jenna's eggs will be the infectious kind." Roache was up to speed as well. "Oh Christ! And judging by how many eggs are on Jenna's back, she'll produce hundreds of the creepy little bastards. I knew there was a reason I've always hated spiders."

Cheavers stopped pacing and took her seat again. "Well, it's a good job Jenna's eggs are unfertilised, don't you think?" Her radio crackled. She picked it up from the table and answered the call. "What is it? I'm right in the middle of some-"

"It's Jenna Martin, ma'am," the soldier's voice replied. "You need to see this."

Rolling her eyes at Aaron, Cheavers got up and beckoned him and Roache to follow her. She informed the soldier she would be there momentarily. "They always need me to see something. None of these people can handle anything on their own. Sometimes, I feel like a glorified babysitter."

Understanding where Cheavers was coming from, Aaron followed her out of the conference room and along the corridor. In the lift, he carried on discussing the situation with his colleagues until they were walking towards Jenna Martin's observation room.

There were three soldiers in full protective clothing inside Jenna's room. Aaron wondered what could have caused such caution. He was handed a suit by a fourth soldier, who handed one each to Cheavers and Roache. Getting geared up took a couple of minutes. When ready, Aaron went through the sterilising gas first. He waited until his colleagues were inside when Cheavers ordered the soldiers to clear the room.

Jenna was lying facing them, her back hidden from view. The poor girl didn't say a word when they walked up to her. Aaron squatted in front of her. Her eyes were open, but Jenna was not looking at him, rather through him. "Jenna? Can you hear me?"

"Oh Shit! Aaron take a look at this," Cheavers suggested.

He had a bad feeling about studying Jenna's body, scared his worst fears might have come true. Getting up, he took his time in bending over Jenna and checking the egg sacs. "Oh fuck, no!" He slapped the hood of his suit in despair. "Please, no, this can't be happening."

The egg sacs were no longer pure white. They had black dots in them, and those black dots kept moving, shimmering. There were over twenty individual sacs on Jenna's back, maybe even thirty. And there were more than one black dot in each sac, maybe three or four dots per egg. "How did this happen?" Aaron felt a bit silly asking the question.

"I think we all know how it happened, Aaron, don't

you?" Cheavers went down to Jenna's level on her knees. "Jenna, honey? Who did this to you?"

Jenna started making a familiar noise in her throat. With her eyes open, but not looking at anything in particular, Aaron wondered if she was asleep? Checking the sacs again, there had to be over a hundred spiders inside the eggs. "I think this is the worst case scenario we were talking about." He received nods from Cheavers and Roache. "So, what do we do?"

"You do what you were brought here to do, Mr. Pike," Colonel Trantor replied, stepping through the doorway wearing a protective suit. "Observe and report."

Anger rose up through Aaron's chest. "You bastard!" He stood up straight before lunging for the colonel, grabbing him by the throat and forcing him backwards until he hit the window. "You told me nothing would happen to Jenna. Look at her, you've just killed that poor girl. What do you think's going to happen when those eggs hatch, hmm? They're going to tear her apart, you fucking psycho."

Aaron managed to finish his tirade just before one of Trantor's soldiers hit him on his shoulder with the handle of a pistol. On the floor, dazed, Aaron glared up at his host. "You're supposed to be protecting these people, not experimenting on them."

Colonel Trantor shrugged Aaron's accusations off.

"We need to study these things, Mr. Pike. It's what this facility is here for. I don't care what you think of me, I do what I do to protect people. The more we know about these things, the easier it will be to destroy them."

"Don't you mean easier to weaponize them?" Roache sneered at the colonel. "Isn't that what you've been ordered to do? You're looking for a way of controlling these things, aren't you? Don't you realise it's impossible? The more they transform, the more they turn into spiders. And spiders can't be trained to kill, colonel."

Aaron found it difficult to hear the exchange between Roache and Trantor because Jenna's purring rose in both volume and intensity. When he turned to face her, the purring stopped, and Jenna sat upright in her bed. "Jenna?"

"He's here!" Jenna got to her feet, the eggs on her back so heavy, she had to bend over slightly to keep her balance. The specially fitted pyjamas she was wearing barely covered anything. She stepped up to the window and started purring.

Colonel Trantor caught Aaron's attention. "What's she talking about? Who's here?"

Shrugging, Aaron regarded Cheavers, Roache, and back to Trantor. "Whoever she's been calling. Colonel, call your people. Tell them to be vigilant. I think we might have a visitor."

Trantor took the radio from his hip and pressed the button on the side. "All level supervisors report in."

One after the other, supervisors contacted the colonel over the radio, each one attesting that everything was fine where they were. All but one. "Level one, do you copy?" There was nothing. No crackly static, nothing. "Level one, come in."

After a few seconds of silence from the staff, a voice came through the radio. "There's something here, colonel. The lift doors are-"

A loud scream down the radio made Aaron jump. The radio transmission cut out, leaving Trantor with a free radio in his hand. "It's one of Hardcastle's offspring, I know it. He's come for Jenna." Another transmission played out through the colonel's radio, more soldiers being attacked by something. Trantor tried to communicate with his soldiers, but they were too busy screaming to reply. "Colonel, we have to hide Jenna."

19

Kyle was sitting on his bed holding five cards. "Earth to Chloe, it's your go." What was with her today? He was getting forgetful himself, but Chloe was taking it a bit far. When he finally got back to bed after visiting with the beautiful Jenna, Kyle had tried to get back to sleep. Slumber had evaded him, though, when he tried to remember his dad's face. For the life of him, he couldn't. Then he tried to recall activities he'd done with his dad. Even that had brought back few memories. Still, his dad's face remained a mystery. "Come on, or they'll be closed." He grinned at Chloe, who was sitting cross-legged opposite him.

"I'm going, don't rush me." Chloe placed a card. "Oh, I'm terrible at this game. Can't we play Snap! or something I'm good at? Pontoon's not my game."

"You're bust now anyway," Kyle replied, laying his winning hand down on the sheet. "We can play whatever you want." He'd decided it was best not to tell his mum about trying to remember his dad, or rather not being able to recall his face. They'd been stuck in the hospital for what felt like a lifetime. Time dragged out in the 'facility'. When he hung his leg over the edge of the bed, a hair dug into him, causing a stabbing pain. "Ouch!" Kyle rubbed his leg, thinking nothing more of it.

"What's wrong, Kyle?" Chloe unfolded her legs and moved from the bed. She squatted in front of him, rubbing his leg. "Let me see, honey."

Pulling his pyjama bottoms down around his ankles, Kyle stood in front of Chloe, feeling her touch. When she rubbed his thigh with her warm hands, he recoiled at the movement in his groin. "Oh, I'm sorry!" He covered his crotch with his hands, praying for it to go down.

Chloe looked up at him and grinned. "Don't be. I'm not." She continued rubbing his leg. "What are these hairs? They're coarser than the others. They're weird, almost like wire."

Bending over, still hiding his manhood, Kyle wanted to be somewhere – anywhere – else. "They're just hairs. Nothing to worry about. Look, mum will be back from the canteen soon. I don't want her coming in and seeing us like this."

"I don't know, Kyle, they feel different." Chloe focused her fingers over one area of hairs, rubbing her index finger over a specific place. "I think I'm going to have to-"

Chloe fell to the floor, like she'd fainted. There was no noise, no grunts, she simply fell like a lifeless doll. Kyle scoffed. "What was that?" He uncovered his crotch, bent down, and lifted his pyjama bottoms, never taking his eyes away from Chloe's unconscious body. "Come on, joker, get up." Going along with the gag, Kyle got down on his knees next to her and started shaking her. "Oh no, please, Chloe. Don't die on me." He chuckled to himself.

When Chloe remained still, Kyle's grin began to fade. It left him entirely in a couple of seconds. "Chloe?" He shook her, harder. "Chloe?" Then harder still. Her eyes were open and lifeless. "Come on, Chloe, if this is a joke, it's not funny." In a couple of movies he'd seen, doctors would put their fingers to a patient's neck to check for a pulse. Kyle tried. There was nothing going on in her neck, not that he knew what he was looking for. "Help! Someone! Help me, please!"

The door hissed open, and Kyle's mum walked in

carrying two polystyrene cups of coffee, one for her and one for Chloe. "Here! I got-"

Desperate for her help, Kyle stared up at his mum. "Mummy, help! She fainted or something. I don't know what to do." Tears streamed down his face as he stroked Chloe's cheek. "Chloe, please wake up."

His mum set the cups of coffee down on the floor beside them. "What happened, Kyle? What was Chloe doing when she fainted?" She put her fingers to Chloe's neck first.

Kyle was panicking. "I-I don't know. I was showing her some new hairs on my legs. She was rubbing them when she fell over." He was fighting back a sob. He wanted Chloe back. "Help her, mum, please."

"I can't feel a pulse, honey." His mum unclipped the radio on Chloe's belt and requested medical assistance at once. "I'm going to have to start CPR, Kyle. Get back!"

For three long minutes Kyle waited for Chloe to come back to life, watching his mum go from compressions to breathing into Chloe's mouth. It was over by the time help arrived. When the door opened, his mum was already exhausted. "It's over. You're too late." Kyle got up and skulked to his bed, where he lay on his side facing the wall. Kyle sobbed.

Chloe's radio crackled behind him. "All personnel to level seven. We have a breach. I repeat, all personnel to level seven. Bring flame units. Do not let the Arachnoid reach this level, is that clear?"

Sitting up, Kyle sniffed the air. An intruder was in the facility. Getting up, Kyle shed his clothes, his mum staring up at him, puzzled. She asked him what he was doing as he ran at the window. Launching himself through the glass, Kyle landed in the corridor, heading for the lift down to level seven. With Chloe gone, he had to protect Jenna.

No one was in the elevator when the doors opened. Kyle stepped on board. On the way down, he hit the stop button, pain wracking his face. "Oh no!" He hit the walls repeatedly with his hands, trying anything to stem the pain. It was behind his mouth. Blood appeared on his fingers. He was bleeding.

Such agony shouldn't be allowed. Kyle fell to his knees clutching at his face when the skin tore. He should have fainted at the pain, but he didn't. Then, as suddenly as the pain started, it stopped. Kyle got up, staring at his reflection in the stainless steel wall. When he glanced down, there was something attached to his face. He touched it. Kyle tried talking, but it came out as a hiss.

He pressed the restart button and a couple of seconds later Kyle was on the seventh level, where soldiers were amassing. Even through the doors screams could be heard. Heading for Jenna's room, Kyle let himself through multiple doors, passing scared soldiers as he went. Some were gung-ho, others terrified.

Jenna's observation room was packed with soldiers, and doctors. Aaron Pike and Dr. Cheavers were present. Cheavers recoiled in shock at his new fangs. Kyle tried to say he was going to kill the intruder, for them to stay back, but it came out as a hiss. The soldiers let him through, making a line to the door.

Soldiers in the next room were being slaughtered by the Arachnoid when Kyle opened the door, walking through the sterilising gas. The Arachnoid finished killing its latest victim, sizing Kyle up. It yanked its clawed leg out of the stomach of some poor soldier.

Kyle went into attack mode, arms reaching out, knees bent. He hissed and launched a web at the beast in front of him. His web missed and hit a wall. The beast, instead of retaliating let off a series of purrs. Kyle understood it. It was asking where Jenna was. Using his throat to purr, Kyle answered it, telling it Jenna was his. She was pregnant with his babies.

The answer angered the beast. It roared and ran at Kyle, its six legs and two arms aiming to end his life. Kyle had speed on his side. When it reached him, Kyle jumped to the side, then launched himself onto its back, wrapping his arms around its head. While it was thrashing about, Kyle was trying to find the best position. When he found it, he sank his fangs into the top of the beast's head, sucking on its lifeforce, feeling it getting slower with every swallow. It took only a minute and a half for the beast to collapse on the floor. Kyle kept sucking, drinking it away, until the taste disappeared.

20

Helen finished telling the soldiers what she knew had happened to Chloe when Kyle started stripping. The call on Chloe's radio sounded serious. "Kyle? What are you doing?" He ignored her, dropping his pyjama bottoms, and revealing how far the infection had spread. Only yesterday his legs had been normal. When he ran at the window, his legs were half grey with black specks. His thighs were covered. "No, Kyle, wait!"

She was too late, her son exploded through the glass, landing on his feet, and heading for the lift. Helen was stunned that he had not hurt himself. Her little boy – or rather fully grown adult man – disappeared from view. "Kyle, wait! Where are you going?"

Feeling bad at leaving the soldiers to deal with Chloe, she headed after her son, who by the time she'd entered the corridor was gone. "Damn it!" At the elevator, she banged on the button, but when she glanced at the display, it said it had stopped. "Come on, you stupid thing." She kept hitting the button.

After three or four minutes, the doors opened, and Helen stepped on board while avoiding the blood on the floor. Selecting level seven, Helen guessed Kyle had to be heading for where everyone else was going. The screaming and noise was palpable when Helen stepped off the lift. She turned and headed for the noise, hoping the colonel had it all under control.

Without being asked to show ID once, Helen reached the busiest room. It was packed with soldiers in their white pyjamas, carrying guns and flame units. Helen recognised Dr. Cheavers and Aaron Pike. Cheavers waved Helen over. "What's going on? What's all that noise?" There was screeching in the next room; it sounded bad.

"You need to tell her, Eleanor," Aaron whispered. "We need to tell her everything."

Cheavers squirmed, trying to get out of it. "Kyle's next door, Helen, fighting that thing."

Smiling, Helen went from regarding Cheavers to Aaron. When they remained serious, Helen's smile dropped. "Fighting what thing?" When Cheavers dropped her gaze and stared at the floor, Helen took a step back. "You mean you let him in there? Why would you do that? He's just a little boy." Of course she realised he wasn't, yet to Helen he was still her ten year-old, who loved playing footy with his mates in the park. Jumpers for goalposts style. "What have you done?" She turned and tried getting through the crowd of soldiers.

Making her way to the door, Helen reached the control pad and put her palm on it. It seemed quiet next door, the screeching having died down. The soldiers surrounding her were keen to find out what had happened. When the door opened and Helen stepped through the sterilising gas, her hands automatically covered her mouth.

Sitting on the floor, Kyle looked up at Helen. Except it wasn't her boy. The face in front of her was not human. It had hideous fangs, like that of a spider, and his body was completely grey with black flecks. The thing he was sitting next to was grotesque in form, like a wrinkly, long dead spider, only huge, five feet almost. Its body was old and dead, dried up like a prune, like something had sucked it dry. And staring at what was once her Kyle, Helen realised that he had killed that beast, had sucked it dry. Helen screamed.

Her son got to his feet and hissed at her. Helen jumped back, when one of the soldiers pointed a flame unit at Kyle. "What are you doing?" She grabbed the flame gun, making sure it was pointing away from her poor son. The soldier protested, but Colonel Trantor intervened. Helen glared at her host. "What have you done to him?"

Trantor shrugged. "Mrs Fisher, you've got it all backwards. We have your son's best interests at heart, I swear. Professor Jackson did this to your son, not us."

In amongst all the soldiers, Aaron Pike appeared. "Come back through here, Mrs Fisher. We'll explain everything, I promise." He beckoned Helen to join him.

Helen glanced over her shoulder at the monster her Kyle had become. He was lost to the world. If he recognised her he didn't show it. If the soldier hadn't intervened with the flame thrower, Kyle might have killed her, too. He might have sunk those ugly fangs into her flesh. Helen nodded, before heading back through with Aaron.

Five minutes later, Helen was back in Kyle's room, the window's glass strewn all over the corridor outside. Joining her and Aaron were Dr. Cheavers and Colonel Trantor. The soldiers were wheeling Chloe's body out on a gurney when they arrived. Trantor was angry and asked what had happened. "She was checking Kyle's new leg hairs out when she just collapsed. I tried resuscitating her, but I was too late." Helen noticed a glance between Aaron and Cheavers. "What? What is it? You obviously know more than you're letting on."

Aaron rubbed his hand through his hair. "Look, Mrs Fisher, it's cards on the table time now, okay? Your son was bitten by a huntsman spider. And now he's turning into one."

Almost snorting in derision, Helen stopped herself, thinking back to Kyle's new fangs. Could Aaron be telling her the truth? "I would say you're having a laugh, but I saw my son just now. What you're talking about is impossible. Tell me how."

Aaron went on to explain the situation, how Professor Jackson and Jonas Eckstein had played God with genetics, testing their theories out on a dozen or so exotic spiders. He explained how he'd found Jackson dead on the ground floor of an abandoned factory, his colleague Eckstein had been sucked of all his bodily juices, like Kyle had done to the beast. Aaron also divulged that a woman, Zoe Hardcastle had been bitten by one of Jackson's test subjects and had gone on to brutally murder at least a dozen people, including a slew of vagrants, who'd been found in the hidden tunnels of Aldwych Station. To add authenticity to his words, Aaron showed Helen the videos he'd down-loaded of Jackson transforming and finally eating Eckstein. "We've had scientists, geneticists here for weeks trying to find out how Eckstein did it, so you see we're still trying to find a cure. It's not over yet."

Aaron was trying to make Helen feel better. "And you're saying my Kyle is going to turn into one of those things?" The videos of Jackson changing were tough to watch. The thought of her son becoming one was terrifying.

With a sigh, Aaron explained. "Not exactly, no. Jackson and Hardcastle were bitten by black widows, Mrs Fisher. Your son was bitten by a huntsman. Kyle is changing, and pretty soon his legs will break off and six new ones will erupt through his ribcage, at which point the spider will be all-consuming."

Helen wanted to burst into tears at the thought of Kyle with legs sticking out of his ribcage, at the thought of Kyle no longer being himself, of the spider taking over his body. If she had not seen Kyle with his fangs earlier, she would have laughed Aaron out of the room. But in the room with Aaron, Cheavers and Colonel Trantor, it seemed all too real. "Okay," nodded Helen, swallowing her fear, "what's next? Where do we go from here?"

No one would answer. Helen went from Trantor, to Cheavers and finally Aaron. "What aren't you telling me? What could you possibly be scared to tell me now?"

Finally Trantor took charge. "There is no next, Mrs

Fisher. There's no cure for what your son has. In a few days his transformation will be complete. We'll be able to study him for a short time once he's fully changed, but after that." The colonel trailed off.

"Yes? After that what?" Helen waited patiently for Trantor to continue.

Trantor cleared his throat. "Well, after that he'll be destroyed."

No, he had to be talking gibberish. "You can't. He's just a little boy. He's just my Kyle. He likes football. He plays in goal. He goes to school and likes drawing. You can't-"

"I'm sorry, Mrs Fisher," Trantor replied, "but it's what we have to face. We have a potential epidemic on our hands. Your son isn't going to be the only bite victim out there. It's my job to make sure this doesn't get out of control. If these genetic anomalies aren't dealt with soon, there's every chance these Arachnoids will be at the top of the food chain. And there's one thing you need to understand, okay? When your son completes his transformation, he won't hesitate in sinking those fangs in you and sucking you dry. In fact, I think he might have attacked you just now."

She wished she wasn't, but Helen found herself nodding. "I know. I don't think he recognised me at all. If your soldier hadn't...I think he would have..."

Aaron stepped up to her and let her use his shoulder to cry on. "I think that's enough, colonel. It's been a lot to take in, Mrs Fisher. Let me escort you back to your room."

Helen didn't argue; instead, she let Aaron lead the way. The last thing she heard was Trantor talking into his radio, telling one of his soldiers to put Kyle in a walled room. Glass windows were not secure, but maybe a two inch thick wall might stop him.

21

Aaron rewound the CCTV footage of Kyle's room for the umpteenth time. He, Trantor and Roache had watched the video of Chloe examining Kyle's leg so many times, they knew every second of it. Aaron pressed play. Kyle dropped his pyjamas bottoms and Chloe started rubbing his leg hairs while they chatted. "I'm telling you it's these new hairs. Chloe didn't just have a heart attack."

"How do you know that, Aaron?" Roache tutted. "I mean, I know she's young, but it's not unheard of, and it's far more likely than Kyle growing lethal darts on his legs."

How could Roache be so blind? "You said it yourself earlier, some spiders grow hairs on their legs that they use as a defence mechanism, right? The hairs irritate their attackers?" He watched as Chloe fell to the floor, while Kyle teased her.

Roache paused the video. "Sure, irritate being the operative word here, Aaron. They rub their legs together and the hairs fly into the air when they sense they're in danger. The hairs don't cause a cardiac arrest. At the most, they might immobilise their prey. You saw that video, Chloe had a cardiac arrest, okay? A simple heart attack."

Pressing play, Aaron snorted. "Simple heart attack? Chloe was in her early twenties with no underlying health conditions. You're telling me you think she just upped and croaked one day? At the exact time she happened to be touching Kyle's leg hairs? Come off it, do me a favour, would you? Why are we even arguing about this anyway? Eleanor will be through with her autopsy any minute. She'll be able to clarify matters."

Trantor's radio crackled to life. "You're going to want to come and look at this, colonel." Unclipping his radio and raising it to his mouth, Trantor pressed the microphone button. "Maybe you can settle an argument, Dr. Cheavers. What's the official cause of death?"

"Officially, it was a cardiac arrest," Cheavers replied, signing off.

When Roache gloated over his apparent win, Aaron switched the monitor off and followed Trantor and

Roache out of Kyle's observation room. He took one last look at the clock on the wall: 20:38. He had not been able to sleep much the past few nights. Aaron would have given anything for a full eight hours of sleep. The lift ride up to level five, where Cheavers was performing the autopsy was a quiet affair, with Roache smirking to himself. A couple of minutes later, Aaron joined Cheavers, Trantor and Roache in the morgue, where Cheavers had Chloe's body laid out on a stainless steel examination table.

The doctor still had Chloe raised, a head block under her shoulders, raising her chest, which made it easier for Cheavers to get to the main trunk of the body. The Y incision had been made. Cheavers had carried out the autopsy and made a good attempt at putting Chloe back together again, minus a couple of organs, which were sitting on a table in front of Cheavers. "Come over here, gentlemen. I've got something to show you."

Still adamant that Chloe had died when touching Kyle's hairs, Aaron sidled over to the good doctor. In front of Cheavers were what appeared to be two human hearts. They looked identical bar one difference. "Is that a hole?" Aaron pointed at the heart on the left.

"We'll get to that shortly." Cheavers picked up the other heart with her gloved hands. "You see this, gentlemen? This is a perfectly normal, healthy-ish heart of a fifty-eight year old male. Take a look for yourself." She showed it to them, one by one, before putting it down next to Chloe's. Then, she picked up the second heart. "This is Chloe's heart." She showed it to them, placing emphasis on the hole in it. "I have to tell you, this is a first for me. In my time as a medical doctor, I've never come across anything like this."

Roache scratched his head. "But you said it was a heart attack, right?"

"Heart attacks don't cause puncture marks like this on the organ, Professor Roache." She put it back down on the table. "Not only did it puncture the heart, whatever this was enlarged it, too, like air had been forced into it or something. Like I said, I've never come across anything like it before. The only saving grace is that Chloe wouldn't have suffered. It was instantaneous. Over so fast, she wouldn't have known anything about it at the time."

"Well, thank God for small mercies at least," Trantor added, crossing his heart like a good catholic would. "Do you happen to have any theories yet?"

"Just the one: I think Aaron's right. I think Chloe touched the hair and it caused this violent reaction. It's the only explanation I have until I've examined Kyle's legs." She took off her gloves and binned them before heading over to a sink to wash her hands. "Believe me, I don't want to get up close and personal with him; there's no telling what's going to happen. Colonel, I'm going to suggest total isolation for Kyle from now on and turn off all fans and shutter the vents in his room. The last thing we want is those hairs getting into the air."

Trantor nodded. "Absolutely. Like you say, the last thing we want is those hairs circulating through the air vents. I've had Kyle placed in a safe room with no glass. Hopefully, he won't be jumping through a two-inch thick wall." He glanced over the two hearts on the table. "That poor girl. Chloe was one of the good ones, for sure. Right, Dr. Cheavers, will you please examine Kyle in the morning? Professor Roache, continue your research into Eckstein's experiments. And Mr. Pike, if you'll follow me, I have a surprise for you." The colonel turned and left the room, closely followed by Aaron.

In the lift going down to level six, Aaron wondered what the surprise might be. There was no point in asking Trantor to give it away; he wouldn't. He walked with the colonel to Kyle's old room, through the observation room and along several more corridors. "Where are we going now, colonel?"

"You'll see!" Trantor remained straight faced.

When they finally arrived at their destination, the colonel opened a door that led to what Aaron took to be a computer room. It had rows of PCs on desks next to one another. Aaron stood by a computer at the front of the room. "I'm confused. What is this place?"

"The comms room," Trantor replied. "This is the only room in the complex with internet connectivity. As a security precaution, we only allow communication in here. Everywhere else is a black spot intentionally. Even the best phone in the world couldn't connect to the internet in any other room." The colonel held the back of a chair. "Have a seat, Mr. Pike. You're going to be thanking me in a minute."

Intrigued, Aaron liked the tone of the colonel's voice. "Right you are." He sat behind the desk and switched on the PC, following Trantor's orders. When he was asked to open Skype, Aaron smiled. He was about to see Lily for the first time in what felt like years. "Thank you, colonel. I appreciate this."

Trantor straightened up behind Aaron. "Right, a couple of ground rules to go through before I let you talk to Lily. Firstly, no talking about where you are. You might not know where we are, but the less time you spend talking about it, the less time you have whispering sweet nothings into her ear. Agreed?" The colonel put his hands on Aaron's shoulders.

"Agreed!" Aaron was too excited about seeing Lily to argue with his host, a man who could make his life miserable if he wanted to. Where they were wasn't even important. Over his time researching Arachnoids, Aaron had reached the conclusion that his work was too important to jeopardise. "Anything else?"

The colonel rattled off a couple more rules before allowing Aaron to open Skype. He almost cried when Lily's pretty face filled the screen. While he was fighting back the tears, Lily let it flow. She'd been so worried about him that she'd almost phoned the police, until the colonel had contacted her telling her Aaron was safe, well and carrying out vital work for the UK's military. "You look so pretty with your hair like that, Lil," Aaron said, sniffing a tear back. "I'm going to be back as soon as I can, okay? And when I do, we're going to take that trip to the Bahamas we've been talking about for so long."

His conversation with Lily took a few minutes. Lily asked where he was once, at which point Aaron changed the subject, asking how her parents were doing. It worked; they started a different conversation that Aaron was grateful for. It didn't matter to Aaron what they chatted about, just seeing her gorgeous smile was enough. Finally, the colonel tapped his watch, listening to them chat. "Hey, Lil, I've got to go, okay? I'm so busy here."

While Aaron was saying his goodbyes to Lily, the

colonel's radio crackled, and Cheavers' voice came over the line. "Colonel Trantor, is Aaron with you? If he is, you'd both better come to Kyle's new room, quick. You'll need to see this." Trantor replied that they would be there soon. "Come on, Mr. Pike, wrap this up. We've got work to do."

It took two more minutes and several kisses to the monitor screen before Aaron let Lily go. When the screen went blank, he wanted to punch it. How long would he be stuck underground for? It wasn't natural to be away from natural light for so long, or to be away from Lily for that matter. They may have been going through a bored patch before Aaron was seconded to Trantor's team, but there was nothing he wouldn't do to get back to her.

Going back over their footsteps, it took a couple of minutes to arrive outside Kyle's room, only instead of a window to observe through, they had a solid wall. Luckily, Cheavers showed Aaron and Trantor what was going on through the camera pointed at Kyle in the next room. They all crowded round the monitor. Aaron went to speak, but Cheavers shushed him.

"Do you hear that?" Cheavers gave Aaron and Trantor questioning glances.

Aaron made a point of listening for a few seconds. "Is that what I think it is?" The doctor raised an eyebrow.

"Is Kyle purring? It's similar to the noise Jenna makes with the back of her throat." He moved in slightly closer to the monitor's speakers. "It is. That's a mating call, I'm sure of it."

"Mating call?" Trantor didn't seem confident. "How can you possibly know that? I mean, Jenna making a call like that I can understand, but Kyle's male, remember?"

"Think about it, colonel," Aaron started. "Jenna was making that noise for days before Zoe Hardcastle's offspring turned up here earlier. She brought him here. And now Kyle's making the same noise."

"Right, so we can expect a visit from a female soon, can we?" Trantor looked to Aaron for answers, then Cheavers.

That was when it struck him. "I don't think we'll need to worry about that." Aaron had to think his plan through for a moment. "Okay, there must be a female out there, right? And as far as we know the only two unaccounted for Arachnoids are Hardcastle's two 'children', one of which was dealt with earlier by Kyle. That leaves just the one female that Kyle's calling to, right?" The colonel and Cheavers exchanged a glance and nodded. "So, why don't we let Kyle out? He'll lead us straight to the female. We can wait until they're both together and destroy them." The doctor and colonel said nothing for a couple of seconds. "Well?"

"I like it, Mr. Pike, except for one thing: Kyle's fast. I mean super-fast. We'll lose him." The colonel seemed keen on the idea. "Unless…No, that won't work."

Aaron jumped on the colonel's hesitance. "What won't work?"

"We could put a tracker under his skin, if we can get to him to sedate him safely." The colonel unclipped his radio, talking to one of his soldiers. "How long do we have before he grows those six new legs, do you think?"

Cheavers shrugged when Aaron regarded her for an answer. "We don't know. Everything's been accelerated with Kyle. Jackson took about four months, I think. Hardcastle I'm not sure about, but with Kyle, I mean, going from a ten year old to twenty in two weeks."

"Your best guess then?" Trantor was insistent on an answer.

"A couple of days, I'd say, maybe three."

Going back to his radio, Trantor chatted to his soldier before clipping it back on his belt. "That's settled. A courier is bringing a tracker here tomorrow lunchtime. Dr. Cheavers will implant the device in the afternoon. If tests are positive, we can have the operation underway the day after tomorrow. Mr. Pike, you and I will be in the air when Kyle leaves this facility, so we'll be in charge of directing the vehicles on the ground."

Aaron was impressed. "That was fast, colonel. This is

a good thing. If we can destroy the female and Kyle at the same time, we'll only need to worry about the infectious spiders Jackson and Eckstein created." He felt the slightest bit guilty talking about destroying Kyle Fisher. It wasn't the lad's fault he'd been bitten by an infectious huntsman. As much as he felt guilty, Aaron had no choice but to destroy him. Arachnoids were the greatest threat humanity had ever faced.

22

TWO DAYS LATER

There was an air of excitement within the Ark. Aaron was excited about breathing real air for the first time since being forced to live and work underground. Even though he would be going straight from The Ark into a waiting chopper, he didn't care. It was better than walking the white corridors wearing pyjamas and nothing on his feet. How he longed to wear socks and trainers again, jeans and an honest to goodness T shirt. Even the soldiers were excited, he noticed, many of their sullen faces replaced with more congenial ones.

The clock on the wall said it was coming up half two in the afternoon. Earlier in the morning, Colonel Trantor had verified that the tracking device implanted in Kyle's neck was working well enough to greenlight the project. Cheavers had successfully implanted the device, while managing to avoid touching any hairs on Kyle's unconscious body. Had Kyle fought his sedation, the project probably would have failed before it had started.

When the door to his room opened, Colonel Trantor joined him. "Are you ready? I have two teams ready to go on our orders. I've given them locators, but they'll need us as their eyes in the sky." He produced a container of pills. "Take one of these if you get airsick. Flying in choppers is a completely different animal to flying civilian style."

Refusing, Aaron couldn't wait to get out of his pyjamas. "I'm fine, really." He followed the colonel to the elevator, where Trantor pressed the button for level one. The journey took a few seconds. When the doors opened, Aaron went with Trantor to a familiar room, where he'd been seen by Dr. Cheavers, strapped to leg braces and subjected to a battery of tests while naked. Why they'd had to run the tests naked, Aaron couldn't fathom, but it was one of the most embarrassing moments of his life.

He could feel he was closer to the surface; the air was different on the first floor, more natural maybe. Or he could have been imagining it. Aaron accepted his old clothes from the colonel, who started undressing, before changing into his green khaki uniform. Handing his pyjamas to Trantor, Aaron changed into his jeans and T shirt, complete with white trainers. Back to normal, Aaron was good to go.

"Remember what I said, Mr. Pike, we're their eyes up there, okay? I need you focused, concentrating. When he gets out, Kyle's going to be fast." Trantor led Aaron to the lift. On board, he pressed the button for the ground floor, freedom.

Trying to relax, Aaron took in a deep lungful of air when he stepped off the lift. It was different, natural. He loved it. There was no way he was going back down there again. Outside of the facility, a helicopter was waiting for them with its propellors whipping up a storm. Aaron couldn't hear anything over the blades until he was sitting inside with a pair of headphones covering his ears.

"This is your last chance for one of these, Mr. Pike." Trantor held out the pot of pills.

When Aaron refused, the colonel opened the tub and popped one in his mouth, putting the packet back in his khaki jacket. The helicopter rose off the ground. Aaron felt his belly plop upon lift off, but it settled once properly in the air.

Leaning in closer while sitting opposite Aaron, Trantor spoke into his microphone. "What can we expect from Kyle? I mean, if he turns while he's out here, what can we expect from a huntsman?" He leaned back after he finished speaking.

The noise of the propellers made Aaron want to shout. "I'm no arachnologist, colonel. I only know what I've researched recently. Huntsman spiders are exactly that, hunters. They don't need big old webs to lure their prey, they actively go out and hunt their food. They're known for their speed and aggression."

Trantor smiled. "So, a thing of nightmares is what you're saying then?"

Unable to disagree, Aaron leaned closer to the colonel. "And I thought the Black Widow was bad. Let's hope we get to Kyle and Hardcastle's baby before he turns."

"Baby? You saw the size of the other one. There was nothing baby size about that."

"And that was the male." Aaron paused for effect. "Female arachnids are almost always bigger than the males. I wouldn't want to come face-to-face with her, I'll tell you that." He glanced out of the window to his right. The facility could have been anywhere, although there were nothing but fields surrounding it, as far as the eye could see. "Where are we anyway?"

The colonel's eyes narrowed. "Well, I guess it can't hurt now." He placed his finger on the microphone, placing it nearer his mouth. "Norfolk. Between the

Robertson Barracks and Norwich. All the Arks were built near army barracks."

Aaron's mouth hung open for a second. "All the Arks? How many are there?" It was news to him, although he wasn't in the know anyway. Why he was surprised was anyone's guess. Nothing should surprise him, not after the past few weeks.

"Five in total. The Robertson Ark is actually the smallest at fifteen levels." Trantor stopped talking when a voice in his earpiece told him they were at the desired altitude. "Excuse me, Mr. Pike. It's time to open the door." He unclipped his radio and held it to his mouth, pressing the button on its side. "We have a greenlight. I repeat, we have a greenlight. Let him out!" He hung off and replaced his radio on his belt. "Now all we have to do is wait."

"Let's hope we can keep up with him." Aaron hoped Kyle wasn't too fast. Even with a tracker implanted in Kyle's neck, they didn't want to lose him. They had a lot riding on Aaron's idea, especially as they were about to release an arachnoid on an unsuspecting population. Still, it was Colonel Trantor who was taking all the risks, not Aaron.

Trantor stared out of the side door window, down at the facility entrance. "We'll keep up with him, don't worry. This baby can fly faster than any animal, mammal or Arachnoid can run, believe me. Maybe you should hope that your theory is correct, hmm? This had better be Hardcastle's baby we're going to meet."

"I'm with you on that," Aaron shouted in response. "I don't see what else it could be, do you? Hardcastle's two are the only ones I know of. At least now we know there's only one after Kyle ate the other one." Aaron checked his watch. Where was Kyle? What was taking him so long? He tapped his wrist, like he was wearing a watch.

"I know." Trantor put his radio to his mouth again. "What's going on down there? Where the hell is he?"

"He's not taking the bait yet, sir," a voice replied. "Oh wait, he's making a move now. He's approaching the door. He's coming your way."

23

Helen should have been banging on the door with her fists trying to get out to see her son, or what was left of him. Instead, she was lying on her bed facing the wall. What was the point? That thing locked in his cell wasn't her son, wasn't her Kyle. The second he'd stood up and hissed at her from behind those hideous fangs Helen had known her son was gone, replaced by a monster. A sob racked her body, her shoulders moving up and down.

The familiar hiss of the door opening broke her sobs. Helen sat upright and turned to face her visitor, who emerged through the sterilising agent as Dr. Cheavers. Through the tears, Helen could tell Cheavers was in a hurry. "What is it?" The doctor was out of breath.

"You ought to know what they're planning, Helen," Cheavers replied, beckoning her to follow. "Come! It's not too late. Kyle's not gone yet."

Confused, Helen got up and ran to Cheavers, who legged it into the corridor. "What did you mean, Kyle's not gone? Gone where?" The good doctor was making no sense. She was trying to keep up with Cheavers, who had longer legs. Helen reached out and grabbed Cheavers' shoulder. She spun her round. "Answer me, damn it! Where's Kyle going?"

"They're letting him go and tracking him, okay?" Cheavers turned and started walking in the direction of the elevator again. "Come on! I'll take you to the control room. We might be able to stop them from releasing him."

In the lift, Helen needed answers. "Why release him? What do they hope to get from tracking Kyle? I'm confused."

The lift stopped, Cheavers got off, waited for Helen to join her, and proceeded toward the control room. "Aaron believes one of the arachnoids is calling for Kyle, like a mating call. He thinks if they release him, Kyle will lead them straight to her. And then-"

Helen did not like the way the doctor let her sentence trail off. "Then what?"

Stopping and turning, Cheavers gave her a sorrowful

expression. "Then they're going to destroy them, Helen. I'm so sorry! Personally, I think they're making a mistake. I tried convincing the colonel to cancel it, but he made me implant the tracker."

She seemed genuine in her sorrow. "It's okay." In that moment, Helen realised the importance of getting to the control room. "We're wasting time standing here like this. Let's go! Move it!" She sprinted ahead, until she had to wait for Cheavers' palm to open a door.

Two minutes later, Cheavers let them into the control room, where a team of soldiers were manning the computers used to control the facility. They had the power to operate all doors, venting, lighting, even oxygen levels. It was a sea of monitors and PCs. The four man team, all wearing their white pyjamas were huddled round a single computer.

"He's not taking the bait yet, sir," a male soldier said into his mouthpiece. "Oh wait, he's making a move now. He's approaching the door. He's coming your way."

Was the soldier talking about her Kyle? It still felt weird calling the twenty-year-old man she didn't recognise Kyle, no doubt, but Helen didn't want him to die. Her poor George. Her husband never got a chance to say goodbye to their son. She followed Cheavers to the group of soldiers, who didn't flinch when they arrived.

The soldier who'd spoken into his mouthpiece

glared up at them. "Dr. Cheavers, why have you brought her here? She's supposed to be holed up in her room." He was about to speak into his microphone when Cheavers leaned over and grabbed the man's pyjama top.

"You're making a huge mistake here, sergeant," she hissed, as the three soldiers with them backed up, shocked at her behaviour. "If Kyle disappears, we've made a bad situation so much worse, do you understand me? If he gets to a female arachnoid and impregnates her, this world of shit we're in right now will feel like heaven by comparison. Now, close the doors. That's a direct order, sergeant. As the facility's physician, I outrank you."

The soldier brushed Cheavers off, standing and glaring at her. "That might be the case if I wasn't carrying out the colonel's direct orders already. If I close the doors, I have to explain to him why I went against his strict instructions."

On screen Helen's son left his room and went into a corridor. The various CCTV cameras displayed on the monitor as Kyle walked, until he reached the elevator she and Cheavers had just stepped off. The soldiers had left the doors unlocked and open, ready for Kyle to escape from. The camera in the lift showed an eager Kyle getting ready to run. His fangs were on display.

Helen wanted to hug him, to tell him everything would be okay, but she knew it wouldn't. Once the colonel achieved his goal, he would kill her boy. "Kyle, come back!"

"Great! Now look what you've done!" The soldier sat heavily on his chair. "Why did you bring her here? Did you think she would convince me?" He tutted. "Sir, he's in the lift. He's reached the ground floor. You should have him in view any second."

The last shot Helen witnessed was of Kyle running across an all but empty car park outside the facility. He sure was fast. If Helen had blinked, she would have missed him.

Regarding Helen, the soldier sighed. "Look, Mrs Fisher, it's not that I wanted to let him go, I didn't, but I have orders. You understand, right? For what it's worth, none of us think this is the right strategy either."

As Cheavers was about to butt in, her radio came to life. "Dr. Cheavers, you need to come see this. Something's happening with Miss Martin." The doctor clucked with her tongue before putting the radio to her mouth. "Copy that. I'm on my way."

The doctor asked Helen to go with her. The journey down to the seventh level took a matter of a few minutes. There were noticeably fewer soldiers about, Helen noted. According to Cheavers, the colonel had ordered twenty-five personnel into vehicles to follow Kyle. Having been warned about Jenna's condition, Helen was hesitant to step into Jenna's observation room. The gas hissed while Helen hesitated.

"You don't have to come in if you don't want to." Cheavers walked through.

Inside, two female soldiers were watching Jenna through the window. "Dr. Cheavers, she started making this noise about five minutes ago." The blonde soldier turned the volume up on the monitor.

The noise was like a deck of cards being flicked, but constant. It was a strange, fast sort of clicking sound. Helen stepped forwards and looked inside with one eye shut. She shut her other eye immediately. The poor young woman's back was like a steep mountain, a bulbous mountain. Instead of flesh coloured, the eggs Jenna was carrying were white with black bits inside, which Cheavers explained were spiders. She didn't dare open her eyes.

"You have Colonel Trantor to thank for this, Helen. These are your son's babies." Cheavers put her hand on Helen's shoulder. "I'm sorry! Not the grandkids you were hoping for, huh?"

"You mean, Kyle and Jenna?" Helen opened one eye a little. It was almost impossible to look at Jenna without feeling nauseous.

"It wasn't consensual, I can tell you that much." The doctor kept watching Jenna. "Trantor let Kyle out of his room one night and led him here. It wasn't his idea; he was just following orders. The powers that be wanted to see what would happen if Jenna's eggs were fertilised, and, well, I guess they're going to get their wish."

"So, what's that awful sound?" Helen put her hands over her ears. With both eyes on Jenna, she felt for the unfortunate woman, whose only 'crime' was having a one-night stand.

Confusion flowed over Cheavers and the two female soldiers, who shrugged. "She's not making that noise with her throat, is she? It's not like her mating call." Cheavers scratched her head. "Gear up, ladies," the doctor said to the soldiers, "we're going inside."

24

"There he is!" Aaron pointed at a small, wooded area beneath them. "I just saw him running between those trees." The colonel gave him a thumbs up and spoke to the pilot through his mouthpiece. "Where the hell are we anyway? We've been flying for ages."

Colonel Trantor listened to his headpiece. "We're somewhere between Colchester and Chelmsford. As soon as Kyle gets to where he's going we'll set down nearby and have to wait for my men to arrive before we engage him."

"Engage him? You mean on foot?" Dread reared its ugly head in his gut. "I thought you were going to blitz them from the sky. You never said anything about soldiers on the ground, colonel. Kyle won't go quietly. Your best bet is to bomb him from above."

With an incredulous glance, Trantor tutted. "What did you think I was bringing my men along for? Sweet Jesus, this is what I get to work with?" The colonel was talking to the pilot about Aaron, rather than to Aaron. "We're not dropping bombs on civilian properties, Mr. Pike." Pointing out of the window, Trantor spoke into microphone. "There he is! I see him. He sure is fast."

Aaron and the colonel had been flying above the streets and countryside for over two hours. When Kyle had raced out of the facility at a rate of knots, they had lost him momentarily, not that it mattered. The tracking device buried in Kyle's neck would have let them know where he was anyway. Aaron had spotted him running on all fours across a main road, narrowly avoiding being hit by a lorry, which had skidded to a stop on the motorway.

The colonel was right: Kyle sure was fast. Given added speed and agility by the arachnid DNA, Kyle was giving the chopper they were in a run for its money. If it wasn't for obstacles in his way, Aaron would have given Kyle the edge. How was he running so fast on his hands and feet? It was amazing to witness.

Checking the surrounding area, Aaron noticed there were a number of farms in the distance. They were flying over a large area of fields and forests. "Kyle spoke to Chloe about some sort of barn in his dream, didn't he?" Trantor nodded. "He might be heading for one of these farms. It looks like he's slowing down." Holding the tracking device's control panel, the speed was decreasing on the display. "What do you think, colonel?"

Taking the panel from Aaron, Trantor read the display for himself. "Let's keep on him. He might be tiring; he's been running like this for two hours and six minutes. That's forty-two miles per hour. Man, that's fast."

The colonel was starting to repeat himself, probably because he was in awe of Kyle's speed, Aaron noticed, taking the panel back. "Yep. He's down to ten miles an hour. Eight. Six." Up ahead, a large farm with multiple buildings and outhouses loomed. Aaron caught sight of Kyle as he emerged from the wooded area. "Two miles per hour. This must be the place." Below them, Kyle went from running on all fours to walking on two legs.

Inside the hovering chopper, Aaron had a bad feeling Zoe Hardcastle's daughter was in one of the barns nearby, calling for Kyle to mate with her. The bite on his chest stung. Massaging it with his free hand, Aaron knew how important it was to destroy her, to destroy them both. On the ground, Kyle stopped outside a huge barn large enough to house several farm vehicles. When Kyle walked inside the building, Aaron suggested that they land in a nearby field.

"Copy that." Trantor ordered the pilot to land. He picked up the radio sitting on the seat next to him. "Sergeant Willis, what's your ETA? Thirty-six minutes? Good enough." He ordered his troops to meet them in the field to the south of the farm.

Wondering how big Hardcastle's daughter would be, Aaron swallowed at the thought of meeting her. He wanted to be anywhere else, at home hugging Lily, at work. Hell, he would take having dinner with his folks over confronting the arachnoid. "I think you're making a mistake with this approach, colonel."

"Duly noted, Mr. Pike." Trantor smiled. "You have nothing to worry about, you know. My soldiers and I have been in tougher spots than this, and up against greater odds, too. When we go to confront them, I'm going to ask that you hang back, okay?"

Aaron almost laughed. "Erm, no problem."

25

Pulling up outside his dad's farm, Quincy Prescott noticed that the house seemed vacant. The biggest give-away being the few pieces of post left on the doormat under the porch. He hoped his old man had not taken a tumble. It had been over a week since he'd spoken to his crank of a dad, who always managed to annoy Quincy whenever they did speak. Since his mum died, his rela-tionship with 'Lance' was strained to say the least.

After exiting his pickup truck on the farm driveway, Quincy checked the front door was locked. He called out for his dad through the door. No answer. Quincy checked none of the bigger windows were unlocked; if one of them was, he might have been able to climb inside. About a month after his mum passed away, Quincy had had a huge row with 'Lance', which had culminated with his dad asking for the spare key back. It would have been handy to have had one to let himself in. "Come on, old man, where are you?"

He tried using his bulk to bust the door down, but it wouldn't budge in spite of his huge six three frame trying to persuade it to let him in. "Damn it! You're starting to worry me now, dad. If you can hear me, yell out. Please?"

With a sigh, Quincy walked round to the rear of the farmhouse, where he found all the windows and doors were locked as well. "Shit!" His dad couldn't be far, his truck was on the drive. He was in two minds whether to call the police or not. While checking the kitchen window, Quincy heard a strange noise.

Turning to the huge old barn his dad used to keep the farm equipment in, Quincy listened. It was strange, like an animal purring, or something. It had to be big to make that kind of noise. "Hello? Dad, are you in the barn?"

Heading in that direction, the sound became louder and louder. "Hello?" What the hell was it? By the time Quincy reached the outhouse, the noise was almost worthy of sticking his fingers in his ears. In addition to the strange purring, Quincy swore a baby was crying inside the barn. He slid the door across slowly, trying not to make too much noise.

The noise stopped as soon as he stepped inside the dark barn. There was movement at the back of the room. "Hello? Dad? Is that you?" He swallowed, the movement getting more pronounced, like someone, or something was getting ready to attack him. To his right, a shovel hung on a hook on the wall. Quincy reached out and grabbed it in both hands. "Whoever you are, I've already phoned the police. They're on their way."

There were several hay bales obstructing Quincy's view. When he passed them with the shovel in hand, two bodies lay encased in some kind of foam, or cloth, or webbing? There was a male and female body, both shrunken and wrinkled, like they'd had their lives sucked right out of their skins.

Distracted by the bodies, Quincy failed to notice the figure behind him. By the time he heard shuffling, it was too late. He turned as something forced him against the wall, covering him in the webbing. Quincy tried moving, but the material was too sticky. Stuck to the wall, covered from head to toe in webbing, the figure stepped up to him. "What the fuck are you?"

With sunlight coming in through the open door, the figure had grey skin with weird flecks of black all over him, like freckles. He was naked, stepping up to Quincy with his manhood hanging between his legs. The freak had fangs or something protruding from his face. The closer the figure grew, the more scared Quincy became.

Behind the figure, a shadow grew in stature, until Quincy recognised the outline. It was a six foot shadow of a spider, except it wasn't a shadow, he realised, when it stepped out from behind some stacked hay bales. Quincy closed his eyes when he could feel the figure's breath. "Please don't hurt me! Please don't hurt me," he kept saying to himself.

The figure's breath went away. Quincy opened one eye slowly. The freak had turned and approached the huge spider. It was stroking the spider's face affectionately. He didn't know what he was watching. And his confusion grew when the spider moved and turned so that its backside was in front of the figure.

Quincy looked away when the figure started moving his hips back and forth. It was fucking the spider with its human organ. "I'm going to throw up."

The figure stopped fucking the spider and let out a pained cry. It pulled out and yelled, falling to its knees before rolling onto its back. Quincy had no idea what it was doing, but it was in pain, he could tell that much. "Please don't hurt me!"

A sickening tear made Quincy nauseous. The freak's legs broke away from its body, leaving only its backside and torso moving. It thrashed around on the ground crying out in pain. The tearing sound was only the beginning. Quincy couldn't unhear the sound of bone breaking as an appendage grew out of its ribcage, long and powerful. The leg moved with the body, until two more burst through its ribs on the right side.

Within a few minutes, the freak had grown three more legs on the left side and lay still, recovering. Quincy swallowed again; he was in the barn with two man sized spiders, one of which had the red markings of the black widow on its underbelly.

After a minute of recovering, the freak got up and crawled on its newly grown legs over to the black widow. Freak mounted her from behind, fucking her with its human genitalia. Quincy was mesmerised, the two monsters mating in such a human way. Fear made Quincy cry out for help. Luckily, his calls went unpunished; the freaks continued mating.

26

Jenna opened her eyes slowly. Lying on her front, she couldn't move. It was like a weight on her back was pinning her to the bed. More alarming than being pinned down was the vibrating inside her. Something was crawling around under her skin. When she tried to lift her head to see what was on her back, the strain was almost too much to bear, but not quite. She managed to catch glimpse of white growths. She gasped. "Dr. Cheavers!"

The door to her room opened as two soldiers in protective suits entered. Jenna hoped one of them was the doctor. They were both female, but not Cheavers. Through the observation window, Cheavers was getting geared up. Using the intercom on the control panel outside, the doctor reassured Jenna that she would be with her in a minute.

"What's happening to me?" Jenna wanted to burst into tears, the things inside her busy moving about, making her skin vibrate. "What are these things on my back?" She took another glance at the white 'cysts', which were not cysts at all.

A sudden pressure built up in the small of her back. It was a familiar sensation, the kind of pressure that she remembered well from picking her spots. When the pressure was at its height, relief swept over her. A warm liquid ran down her skin, followed by the pitter patter of tiny legs. It tickled.

The two female soldiers stopped. They were too busy flapping about some spiders creeping their way toward them to help Jenna. "Doctor Cheavers, what do we do? They're hatching! They're all hatching?"

Why was the soldier pointing at Jenna and saying, 'They're hatching'? "What's hatching?" More pressure built up in her back, followed by liquid dribbling down her and the tickling sensation of little legs or something. More spiders appeared on the floor, creeping toward the soldiers. There were about ten spiders in total. Where were they coming from? And why were the soldiers so scared of them?

Outside, in the observation room, Cheavers leapt at

the control panel and the doors closed suddenly, leaving the two soldiers in there with Jenna. Fear only hit Jenna when the soldiers ran over to the door and started banging on it, trying to flee. "Hey, where are you going?" Jenna tried to lift her body weight, to get off the bed. "Please, don't leave me here."

The soldiers were screaming to be let out, still banging on the door, when the spiders advanced on them. One of the soldiers turned and faced the spiders. She backed up to the door, her arms splayed out. "Dr. Cheavers, open this door! Now!"

"I can't do that. I'm sorry!" Cheavers backed away from the control panel.

The soldiers glared at Jenna, when one of the small spiders shot a web out at them. The soldier with splayed arms screamed when the web hit her visor. The visor started steaming, the plastic cracking. The soldier whipped off her hood, leaving her exposed to the elements. She dropped the visor when another spider shot a web in her direction. It hit her cheek, immediately causing a melting reaction. The soldier screamed, clutching at her face. The web started eating away at the flesh of her hand.

Jenna screamed at the sight of the soldier's skin eroding in front of her. More pressure built up in her back, which meant only one thing: more pain was on its way. The pressure was more intense and covered her entire back.

Screaming forced Jenna to look up. Spiders were crawling up the soldiers' legs. They were bending over, trying to flick them off. "Dr. Cheavers! What's going on? Why is this happening?" A couple of the spiders spat webs at the window. The glass started steaming and cracking.

The pressure peaked. Liquid ran down Jenna's back. When she craned her neck to look behind her, Jenna almost puked when a spider crawled out of one of her 'cysts'. They weren't cysts at all; they were eggs. Spiders, too many to count crawled out of her back, down the covers onto the floor, where they joined their brothers and sisters in attacking the soldiers. Jenna was some kind of sick host for the spiders, she realised, screaming.

27

Helen had to avert her eyes when Jenna's eggs hatched almost simultaneously. The poor girl's back was red raw and bloody. There were so many spiders climbing out of the eggs. The arachnoids were ganging up on the soldiers Cheavers had locked inside Jenna's room, crawling all over them. The window was cracking from the inside, the steam making it damn near impossible to see what was going on. Keeping her eye on a bottom corner of the window, Helen motioned for Cheavers to join her. The spiders were climbing a wall, onto the ceiling. "They're using their webs to burn a hole in the ceiling, look!"

Awed by the intelligence of the spiders, Cheavers called out for help over her radio. "We have a security breach on level seven. All personnel come to level seven. Bring flame units."

Flamethrowers should do it. Helen started climbing out of the protective suit she was halfway putting on. "What are we going to do if they get through that ceiling, Eleanor?" How were these things smart enough to know what to do? Then Helen supposed they were human in some small way, too, except they were far more spider in both appearance and behaviour.

"We can't let that happen, Helen," Cheavers replied, waiting by the door for help to arrive. "If these guys get here in time, they just need to torch these things and it will be over."

Spiders were still hatching out of Jenna's back. Instead of a mountain of eggs, Jenna's body was almost the right size, only there was a huge crater in her flesh. The poor woman was still alive, Helen noticed. "We have to do something to help Jenna. She's in so much pain. This is too much." Tears ran down her cheeks.

"As soon as these guys get here, they'll help Jenna, I promise."

The way the doctor's sorrowful eyes locked with Helen's, made her confused. "Help how?" It didn't take long for the answer to present itself. "You mean kill her, don't you?" Helen took one last look at Jenna lying on her bed, blood dripping on the floor. "Surely there's something else we can do, isn't there?"

Cheavers shook her head. "Can you see her coming back from this?" More spiders emerged from the bloody mess that was Jenna's back. "No, the most humane thing to do would be for us to ease her suffering, Helen."

The spiders had made a hole big enough in the ceiling for them to crawl through. "Quick! They're getting through!" Helen used her palm to open the door. Three soldiers carrying guns and flame units joined them, barging Helen out of the way. "Kill the ones on the ceiling first. They can't escape from here."

"Don't tell me what to do, lady," the first soldier said, trying to get a glimpse through the cracking glass. "Oh shit! They're already through." The soldier in charge ordered his two subordinates to enter Jenna's room and take out the remaining arachnoids. They weren't dressed for combatting the spiders, wearing only their white pyjamas and no footwear.

Helen had not worn clothing on her feet since she'd arrived. Walking round barefoot was second nature, but when the subordinates opened the door to Jenna's room, she hunted for foot protectors. There were none. Giving up, Helen watched through the window.

Spiders on the ground chased the soldiers as soon as they set foot inside the room. They didn't get a chance to use their flamethrowers. The spiders shot acid webs at the two unsuspecting military men, both of whom lost limbs when the webs sliced through their flesh, leaving arms and legs on the floor. The pair were left screaming when the soldier in charge closed the door, sealing their fates.

The window continued cracking, as the arachnoids spat more webs at the glass. Helen stood back when the glass finally shattered, leaving them prey to the arachnoids. About to leg it to the door, a soldier outside used his palm to close it, sealing them inside. The soldier in charge tried the opposite door, but it wouldn't open. "Shit! We're locked in here."

Arachnoids were climbing the walls, lining up to escape through the hole in the ceiling. Helen's hope at escape dashed, she wanted her final acts to be kind, meaningful. She wanted to help Jenna, who was screaming in agony next door. When the arachnoids started climbing through the shattered window, into their room, Helen stood back against the wall. "What do we do now?"

The soldier in charge aimed the flamethrower at the arachnoids advancing toward them. Before he could pull the trigger, one of the arachnoids spat a web at his shoulder. The web burned through his flesh, as the weapon dropped to the floor, his hand and arm still attached to it. The soldier screamed when the spiders started climbing up his legs. He had no more weapons. With only one arm remaining, what could he do? He cried out when one of the arachnoids bit him. The rest then climbed back down his leg, along the floor and back into Jenna's room. "What? That's it?"

Helen was trying to avoid a cluster of arachnoids aiming for her. There was nowhere for her to go except along the wall. Too late, an arachnoid reached her foot, climbed on and bit her big toe. It then climbed back into Jenna's room, joining the queue to leave. "They don't mean to kill us at all. They just want to bite us."

"Yeah? And make us one of them." Cheavers was still trying to avoid being bitten. "That's as good as dead if you ask me. I don't want to be like Kyle, I don't want to be a fucking huntsman. Or a black widow for that matter." The spiders were matching Cheavers' efforts to avoid them, reaching her. One bit her on her ankle. "Well, shit!"

Helen was dead. All three of them were. If they lived for long enough they would all start to change, growing in strength, turning grey, until they sprouted fangs and started eating people. Eventually legs would erupt through their ribcages and their real legs would snap off. Helen had to cover her face with her hand to stifle a sob. No, they couldn't live.

The soldier in charge used his remaining hand to use his radio. "Colonel Trantor, we have a breach on level seven, sir. Please advise." The radio stayed silent for a few seconds. The colonel asked how bad the breach was and if it could be contained. "No, sir, the breach is total. Shall we move to Plan B?" The colonel replied in the affirmative after a lengthy pause. The soldier changed frequencies. "The colonel has given the greenlight to operation firebomb."

28

Colonel Trantor clipped his radio onto his belt, not looking Aaron in the eye. "Where the hell are they? They should be here by now, damn it!"

Aaron had heard the sergeant talking over the radio. The Ark had been breached by Jenna's offspring. That must have meant a few of the colonel's men had been killed. "Plan B, colonel? What's that?" He tried to be as calm as he could when he spoke.

"Shit! I knew this would happen," the colonel replied, his hands on his head. "The Ark is damaged goods, okay? With the arachnoids running around down there, Plan B is our failsafe. It's the only way to be sure we destroy them all." Trantor took a deep breath.

Getting up from the edge of the doorway of the

chopper, Aaron had a feeling he knew what the colonel's Plan B was. "So, what, you're going to blow it up?"

"Operation Firebomb, uh-huh!" The colonel nodded gravely. "All that time spent on digging it out, getting the DNA samples stored, gone. It's all gone in the push of a button."

It was Aaron's turn to take a deep breath. "Shit! I thought you said you don't go around dropping bombs on buildings anyway."

"Civilian buildings, no," Trantor corrected. "The Ark is a military installation. We can make up any story we want, and no one will challenge us. If we just dropped a bomb on this farm, well, you can imagine the shit we'd get for that." The colonel unclipped his radio and was about to speak when engines made themselves known. "It's about bloody time."

Stepping up to Trantor, Aaron put his hand on the colonel's chest. "How long do your men have down there, hmm? How long do they get before the bomb drops?" He hoped and prayed Helen, Eleanor and Jenna made it out in time. If he'd had his phone, he would have called the doctor.

"About ten minutes, okay?" Trantor shrugged Aaron off and started walking towards his troops approaching in their army vehicles. "Do yourself a favour and focus on the job at hand, Mr. Pike. We have our own problems to deal with, like killing these fucking things."

The soldiers parked their Jeeps and Humvees in the same field the pilot had landed the chopper in. Luckily, it was a pretty remote area with lots of surrounding fields. The soldiers all gathered carrying their machine guns around the helicopter, waiting for the colonel to start his speech. Aaron sat on the edge of the chopper, while Trantor gave it, telling his men why they were there and what the challenge was.

Once satisfied the soldiers were briefed, the colonel ordered them to approach the big barn to the farm to their east. His men obeyed, starting their approach. Aaron followed slightly behind Trantor, the only civilian there, the only person not carrying a weapon. If something went wrong, Aaron was unprotected.

The closer he came to the barn, the greater his fear rose. By the time the barn was in clear view, Aaron wanted to pack up and go home to Lily. If only, What he would have given to have held her in that moment. The colonel put his fist up, clenched, warning him to stop.

Three soldiers ran up to the barn door and opened it. They backed away when something screeched inside the outhouse. With their guns ready, the doorway remained empty. One of the soldiers went ahead, his machine gun poised.

Something was wrong. Without warning, the soldier on point fell to the ground. His knees didn't bend and his arms didn't go out to limit damage either. The two soldiers in the rear went to his aid. Aaron could only think of one person in that moment: Chloe. "Kyle's using his hairs!" He shouted at the top of his voice.

His warning came too late. The two soldiers trying to help their brother-in-arms fell beside the point soldier. They didn't stand a chance. The poison darts that were Kyle's hairs caused a massive coronary in everyone they touched.

"There it is!" A soldier yelled up ahead.

A huge form appeared in the doorway. It was Kyle in all his grey, six-legged, two armed glory. Aaron took a step back at how big Kyle was. The boy was a six foot Huntsman-human hybrid. With a growl, Kyle started rubbing his rear legs together. "Colonel, he's releasing hairs into the air." Aaron tried to wrap himself up in his clothing.

The soldiers let rip with their guns, mostly hitting the wood of the barn. Kyle was too fast for them. A couple of Trantor's men fell to their deaths without firing a shot. Kyle managed to dodge the bullets, grabbing one soldier, and sticking his fangs into the man's skull. Cleverly, Kyle used the dead soldier as a shield against the soldiers' onslaught. It was a slaughter. Kyle attacked the soldiers one-by-one, taking them out. Some he fired acidic webs at, slicing off appendages. One soldier was sliced in half at the waist. He tried crawling away, leaving his bum and legs behind until he succumbed to blood loss and shock.

Trantor kept back, firing in Kyle's direction. It was chaos. It was carnage. Kyle was too fast. By the time the soldiers had trained their guns on him, Kyle was off in a different direction. Aaron stayed behind the colonel, who kept swearing when Kyle attacked another of his soldiers. There were only a handful left.

With guns going off sporadically around him, Aaron found a small outhouse, used to store a sit-on lawn-mower. While the colonel and his men were trying to take out Kyle, he was opening the outhouse door and hiding inside. When Aaron watched through the gaps in the wooden slats, there were two soldiers and Trantor.

The soldiers made a shield around the colonel. Kyle approached them slowly, sizing them up. Aaron prayed one of them shot Kyle. The arachnoid was so close to him, too close. "Come on, guys, fucking shoot!"

When the two soldiers fired at Kyle, the arachnoid had already made his move, the bullets missing him by a considerable measure. Kyle tore both soldiers apart using his spear-like legs to skewer them, before pulling them apart one-by-one. The colonel was the only person standing between Aaron and Kyle.

Swallowing his fear, Aaron opened the door and came out with his hands raised. "Kyle! I know you can hear me. It's me, it's Aaron, remember?" He'd tried reasoning with Zoe Hardcastle down in the bowels of Aldwych Station. That had not ended well. Aaron's only hope was that Kyle's personality remained in there, somewhere.

Aaron soon learned it wasn't. Kyle hissed and shot a web at Trantor's neck. It latched onto it and when Kyle yanked on the web, Trantor's head separated from his body and fell onto the earth at Aaron's feet. Trantor's eyes were looking up at him, they blinked twice, and the colonel tried to say something when his eyes went blank, and he died.

Kyle was facing Aaron. Colonel Trantor's machine gun was on the ground next to Aaron. It was the only weapon he had against his much stronger foe. If he could get to it, he might have stood a chance.

Too late. When Aaron dived for the gun, Kyle spat a web at him. It hit Aaron's knee, wrapping itself round the top of it. The melting started immediately. Aaron screamed in pain, reaching for the machinegun. His flesh melted until his leg came away, leaving Aaron with a stump cut above the knee. He was done for. Kyle crept slowly towards him.

Reaching the gun, Aaron picked it up and rolled onto his back. Kyle screeched and rushed him, hovering above Aaron, ready for the kill. Aaron held the gun up and pulled the trigger, a burst of five rounds hitting Kyle's chest.

The arachnoid fell and rolled. Kyle backed away, hurt. Sitting up, Aaron pointed the gun at Kyle and pulled the trigger again. Eight bullets hit Kyle in the face, destroying it. Kyle lay on his back with his six legs curled inward.

Aaron dropped the machinegun, clutching at his stump. It was still steaming when another screech caught his attention. Zoe Hardcastle's daughter emerged from the barn. She was about to attack Aaron when he reached for the gun again.

Zoe's daughter stopped, checked behind her, turned and ran in the direction of some woods behind the farm. Aaron was sweating profusely. He felt sick. The wound wasn't bleeding, as the acid had cauterized it. He wasn't in danger of dying of blood loss. It was the pain. He crawled over to the colonel's headless body and found the radio.

29

"Hey, you know what to do. Professor Roache is the only one here with ground level clearance," the soldier in charge said, holding the radio with his only hand. "Oh God, I feel faint. I think I'm going to throw up." He steadied himself by leaning against the door. "You have to get Roache out of here, okay? He's the key to ending this. Roache is the only one who knows what those machines do. Promise me you'll get him out of here, and yourself."

"But Vic," a female voice crackled, "I can't leave you here. I'll get help."

Helen wanted to look away, but she couldn't. The soldier, Vic, sunk to the floor slowly, eventually sitting down, still leaning against the door. Her heart was breaking for him.

"Siobhain, don't, please. Focus on the mission," he said, deflated. "I've been bitten, baby. Even if I get out of here, in a few weeks I'll be one of these things. No, we need to stay down here, okay? Please, just go and get Roache."

Staring through the doorway into Jenna's room, Helen tried not to interfere with their 'moment'. It was obvious to her that Vic and Siobhain were a new couple, probably since being forced to stay in the Ark. Jenna was sobbing on her bed, blood dripping on the floor below. The last of the spiders were crawling up the wall and along the ceiling to the hole they'd made.

"Fine, I'll go!" Siobhain snapped. "But as soon as Roache is safe, I'm coming back for you, okay? I don't want any arguments."

It was an empty promise. Everyone stuck in Jenna's room knew it, except Jenna, maybe, who was too busy sobbing to know what was going on. Happy that Vic wasn't about to faint, Helen made her way inside Jenna's room, where Dr. Cheavers was sitting with her back to a wall, a blank expression defying what must have been going on inside her head.

Vic and Siobhain said their goodbyes in the background, all the 'I love yous' that Helen wanted no part of. Helen went and sat with Jenna, holding her hand. "It'll all be over soon, Jenna. I promise." She wasn't sure if Jenna had heard them talking about the bombs about to be dropped on them. They had spoken at length about Operation Firebomb, but Jenna had been crying for the entirety of the conversation. Even saying those words in her mind sounded alien. She, Jenna, Cheavers and Vic were about to die, blown up by the powers above, dropping a bomb on them. All of a sudden, Helen needed to pee.

"Kill me, please," Jenna pleaded, her sobbing subsiding. She shrugged off Helen's hand and pointed at the flamethrower on the floor. Vic's arm was attached to it. "Please, end it. I'm in so much pain. I just want it to stop."

"And it will, soon, Jenna," Helen said, moving in closer to her. "You don't want me to use that. It's a flamethrower, honey."

Jenna nodded. "I know...What it is. Please, you're Kyle's mum. Please, Helen, I don't want to wait ten minutes. Please...I beg you."

Helen went to Cheavers for help. The doctor shrugged and got to her feet. When Cheavers stooped and picked up the flamethrower, Helen got up and met her by the door. "What're you doing? Put that back down." Cheavers peeled Vic's finger from the trigger and dropped the arm on the floor.

"Who are we to deny Jenna her last wish, huh? We're

all dead now, Helen." Cheavers held the weapon and aimed it at Jenna while talking. "If I could kill myself, I'd do it right now, but I can't. I'm a coward, so I'll have to wait until the bombs drop and we're turned into dust. But Jenna, we can ease Jenna's suffering. Don't you see?"

"How? By burning her to death? Do you know how painful that will be?" Helen couldn't fathom the immense pain Jenna would feel. It made her shudder.

"No more painful than now." Jenna winced and burst into tears.

The poor girl's back was raw and bloody. There was a huge crevice where her muscles and cartilage had been and from where the spiders had hatched. They were right, though. Who was she to deny Jenna's dying wish? "If you do this, fry those little fuckers up there while you're at it." She pointed up at them crawling through the hole one by one. "You won't get them all, but you might get a few."

Cheavers nodded, before tightening her finger on the trigger. Helen stood back, bumping into Vic, who put his hand on her shoulder from behind. She covered his hand with her own. "I'm so sorry this happened to you, Jenna. I'm sorry it happened to all of us."

There was no warning. Cheavers let a long line of flame cover Jenna and the bed. She left it going for thirty seconds before turning the weapon onto the ceiling and covering the last of the straggling spiders. Jenna screamed in pain for a full minute, which was all Helen heard. Luckily for her, Jenna's screams wouldn't haunt her for long.

When Cheavers finished burning the ceiling, she dropped the flamethrower and joined Helen and Vic in the observation room. Smoke was billowing in. The ceiling was ablaze. Vic's radio came to life.

"We're all out, Vic. There's no time to come and get you. I'm so sorry, the plane's almost here. I can hear it coming." The female soldier burst into tears down the line, trying to say something that her sobbing muffled.

"Good, honey, it's the way it should be." Vic let the radio fall into his lap. When Siobhain tried to talk to him, he threw the radio to the other side of the room.

They were seconds away from the end. Helen was sitting with Cheavers one side and Vic the other. She reached out with both arms and pulled them both in for one last huddle. There was nothing left to say. She kissed Cheavers on the side of her head, then Vic.

A loud thud above them made Helen stare up at the ceiling. There were so many things she wanted to do. All she wanted was to cuddle George one last time. And her Kyle. Tears ran down her cheeks as rumbling grew in intensity and volume until the ceiling collap...

30

A WEEK LATER

Captain Marcus Callow put his fist up to stop his men from talking. He and his squad had been hunting the damn arachnoids for weeks with no luck. He'd been given orders to search every abandoned subway tunnel, but Marcus was losing hope of ever finding any. The newspapers and news channels went into a frenzy over the bombing of a military installation in Norwich, every journalist speculating over the cause. Officially, the RAF had claimed a faulty part on one of their planes had released the bomb on a routine fly-over. What did they know?

Unofficially, and known to his squad, the bomb had decimated The Ark, four people and a whole load of arachnoids. Boom! Operation Firebomb had saved hundreds, maybe even thousands of lives, not that the public would ever know. Since Colonel Trantor's demise at the hands of the little boy who'd been bitten by a huntsman spider, Marcus' new commander was Colonel Ernest Langley. His squad were rightly spooked at hearing how the huntsman had taken out twenty-five fully trained soldiers in less than five minutes. The bloody thing had decapitated Trantor.

"Captain, what the fuck are we doing down here?" Sergeant Badcock was on one knee, his machinegun aiming down the tunnel, ready for action. "You know those things can just let off a bunch of hairs and we're fucking dead, right?"

Marcus understood Badcock's fear. His squad of six all understood it, since helping to clear up the bodies at the farm. Some of the corpses were intact; they could have been lying on the job. The others, though, they'd been brutally torn to pieces. Even the civilian, the entomologist had sustained injuries; he'd lost his leg in his fight against the huntsman. Marcus had to give the civilian credit where it was due: he'd blown the huntsman away. But, the female arachnoid was still at large, and more than likely pregnant.

A couple of his guys started talking when Marcus silenced them. A scream. It was a woman's scream further down the tunnel. They were in the Marlborough Road subway, going from room to room, corridor to corridor, checking for arachnoids. "You all heard that. Someone needs our help." He ordered Badcock to take point.

With torches on their helmets and the ends of their machineguns, Marcus went with the rest of his squad until the scream was loud. Inside an empty room that stank of piss, a woman was lying on her front, screaming. When Marcus passed his torch over her back, it was red and moist. "Holy shit!"

"Just kill me, please!" The woman didn't look up at him.

He jumped when a spider crawled out of the bloody mess that was once her back. It looked like there should have been more of the little critters. It was a lot of mess for just one. But where were they?

Marcus shone his flashlight above him. The whole ceiling was covered with spiders. Falling to the ground, pointing his gun up, Marcus realised it was futile. Bullets wouldn't do anything. "Badcock, use the flamethrower! Quick!" His sergeant was not quick enough. By the time the weapon had been drawn, acidic webs had decapitated Badcock. The rest of the squad panicked and fled, leaving Marcus with a room full of arachnoids.

He'd not noticed spiders on the ground until something tickled his neck. Before he could flick it off, the little bastard bit him. After he'd been bitten, the other aggressive spiders seemed to ignore him. They turned and headed out into the corridor, after his squad. "Hey guys!" Marcus got up and hurried into the corridor, where his squad were on the floor covered with arachnoids.

Thinking they'd been killed, Marcus' hope abandoned him for a moment, until the arachnoids moved on, leaving his guys alive. "Are you all alright?" The rest of his team confirmed they were. He stared down at the bite mark on Wyatt's arm. "Was everyone bit?" One by one they nodded and showed their wounds. He stood up straight and watched the arachnoids crawling away. "Fuck! I have to call this in."

Wyatt put his hand up. "Whoa! Wait a minute, captain. Please, you can't report this." He gestured the bitemark on his arm. "You know what happens to bite victims as well as I do. I can't be put in quarantine, sir. Please."

The rest of his team agreed. Marcus didn't like the thought of turning himself over to the science guys either. What little time he and his squad had left should be theirs to do with as they pleased. The others pleaded with him. "I'm probably going to live to regret this, but." He unclipped his radio. "This is Captain Marcus Callow.

Yeah, we're gonna need assistance down here. I have one man down. I repeat one man down. The threat is over, but quarantine measures will need to be put in place, over."

"How the fuck is that helping, sir?" Wyatt rubbed his stubbly hair, agitated.

"Watch your tone there, Wyatt. I'm the fucking captain here, remember! And I haven't given us up yet, have I?" The longer Wyatt was on his team, the more confident and aggressive he became. Marcus had to bring him down every now and then. "You're all lucky I've got commitments I can't get out of, otherwise I would be placing us under quarantine. But hey, I figure we've got maybe a few weeks until we start changing into these things. I suggest you use this time to wrap things up with your families and friends, okay?" Marcus started scratching his neck, knowing the infection was snaking its way into his system. Pretty soon, he would be the one being chased by men with guns and flamethrowers.

If you enjoyed this book, Raven Tale Publishing has a reader group, where you will meet other readers, be in with a chance of winning paperbacks, ebooks and other

assorted goodies, and you'll be invited to join our ARC group, too. Simply click on the link below:
Raven Tormented Readers | Facebook

You can also follow D.C. Brockwell here:
Facebook: DCBrockwell Author | Facebook
Instagram: Duncan C Brockwell (@dcbrockwell) • Instagram photos and videos
Twitter: @dcbrockwell1

Printed in Great Britain
by Amazon